COCK OF THE WALK

THE POPE "TRYING IT ON" MR. JOHN BULL.

Punch warns easy-going John Bull and the somnolent
British lion to wake up before they are topped by
Cardinal Wiseman's hat.

ROY LEWIS

COCK OF THE WALK

*   *   *

A MID-VICTORIAN RUMPUS

PETER OWEN

LONDON & CHESTER SPRINGS PA

PETER OWEN PUBLISHERS
73 Kenway Road London SW5 0RE
Peter Owen books are distributed in the USA by
Dufour Editions Inc. Chester Springs PA 19425–0007

First published in Great Britain 1995
© Roy Lewis 1995

ISBN 0–7206–0942–9

A catalogue record for this book is available
from the British Library

Printed and made in Great Britain by
Biddles of Guildford and King's Lynn

PREFACE

Most history is a mixture of facts and fiction. Conjecture, interpretations, explanations of historical facts or events in the past are all matters of degree. The raw facts of history (which includes of course biography and archaeology) are artefacts, written, printed or incised records, letters and archives, human remains. On these rest the superstructure of history, whether the most 'scientific' of scholarly elucidations or some degree of 'fictional' development of the evidence.

This reconstruction of a peculiar episode in English social and religious history combines both elements: that which is on record, and that which is conjectural and selective. I have used as the basis of the story the historical 'facts', as recorded in contemporary newspapers, *The Times, the Morning Post, The Illustrated London News, Punch,* and a few others. Of the other records I have consulted, for example, Hansard, the Annual Register, Debrett, Bradshaw. My research into the 'events' goes no deeper than this: making a serviceable but not exhaustive record, such as theologians would ask for, ignoring mere personalities, all of which are fictional though in no case fictitious. To introduce to the reader the full *galère* of the actors and actresses of the play (some episodes in history are, fortunately, 'as good as a play'), I have read the written evidence in the form of the memoirs and (sometimes at second hand) recollections of what happened and what those concerned felt about it, often some time after the circumstances were put in the storage disks of memory. These range from Charles Greville's *Memoirs* to Queen Victoria's *Journal*: not to bore the reader over-curious of separating semi-fact from pure invention, some dozens of them.

So what about the pure fictions in the tale? Well, these are creations of the 'it must have been like this' variety: mostly, in truth, the real guts of history – the conversations, the talk, the exclamations, the feelings, even the Freudian slips, of those involved. In an historical novel *per se* the author is practically fancy-free; more anchorage is required within an inelastic timetable and scenario. One tries to catch the 'spirit of the thing' here and there. To achieve this, one may even adjust, a little, the precise order of events (though naturally not of Cabinet meetings) rather in the way Beerbohm's Architect of the Universe considerately adjusted the cloud pattern over Oxford to accommodate the aesthetic preference of Zuleika Dobson's ill-fated lover.

ROY LEWIS

CONTENTS

Dramatis Personae	9
1	13
2	18
3	24
4	31
5	36
6	44
7	48
8	58
9	64
10	70
11	73
12	80
13	84
14	88
15	97
16	103
17	107
18	111
19	116
20	122
21	125
22	132
23	138
24	142
Some Years Later	151

Illustrations reproduced from *Punch* appear on pages 2, 15, 27, 41, 53, 65, 79, 91, 105, 117, 129, 141.

Pride in their port, defiance in their eye,
I see the lords of human-kind pass by.

Oliver Goldsmith, *The Traveller*

DRAMATIS PERSONAE

None of the characters who play a part in this historical narrative is imaginary. Any parallels with contemporary people or events are coincidental.

Queen Victoria and Albert, Prince Consort
Earl of Aberdeen, Tory Opposition leader
Giacomo Antonelli, papal secretary
Dr John Ashburner, MD
Charles Babbage, inventor
The Revd Charles and Mrs Brookfield
Thomas Carlyle, writer and prophet
Jane Welsh (Mrs Thomas) Carlyle
John Thaddeus Delane, editor of *The Times*
Duke of Devonshire
Benjamin Disraeli, Tory leader in the House of
    Commons
Mary Anne (Mrs Benjamin) Disraeli
Mary Ann Evans (later George Eliot)
W.E. Gladstone, 'Peelite' leader
Sir James Graham, Bt, MP
Holman Hunt, Pre-Raphaelite painter
The Revd Charles Kingsley, socialist parson, writer
Mark Lemon, editor of *Punch*
George Henry Lewes, writer
Karl Marx
Henry Mayhew
Giuseppe Mazzini, Italian patriot
John Everett Millais, Pre-Raphaelite painter
Monckton Milnes, MP
Fr John Henry Newman
Florence Nightingale

Hon. Mrs (Caroline) Norton
Lord Palmerston, Whig Foreign Secretary
Coventry Patmore, poet
Joseph Paxton, architect
Pope Pius IX
Augustus Pugin, architect
Dante Gabriel Rossetti, Pre-Raphaelite painter and poet
Lord John Russell, Prime Minister
Lady Russell
Colonel Sibthorpe, MP, curmudgeon
Elizabeth Siddall, model
Herbert Spencer, philosopher
Lord Stanley, Tory Opposition leader
Miss Augusta Talbot, an innocent
Alfred Tennyson, Poet Laureate
William Makepeace Thackeray, novelist
Lord Truro, Lord Chancellor
Samuel Wilberforce, Bishop of Oxford
Cardinal Wiseman

1

That afternoon His Holiness was in a relaxed mood designing railways.

Outside the Vatican the weather was still on the hot side, and lady tourists were advised not to attempt the full tour of the Aurelian walls – especially the Gianicolo – to observe the sites where the Roman Republic had been so nobly, if vainly, defended by Mazzini and Garibaldi against Oudinot's zouaves; but young Hallam was there, scratching his mosquito bites and noting the rudeness of the Romans to passing clerics. As an alternative, a visit to St Peter's was recommended to English visitors.

The Pope's study was probably just as cool.

The Secretary of State was admitted reluctantly.

'Ah, Giacomo, my dear friend,' said the Pope, bidding him rise. 'Not more foreign affairs today, surely? Now, just look here at the map. The distance from Rome to Civita Vecchia is sixty-two miles by the Via Aurelia, and it's an infernally bad road at that. But it's so flat that the rails can follow it closely all the way with little need for expensive cuttings or embankments. Or bridges. A few level crossings will serve where road and rail cross. There will be signals to warn and the engine will whistle.'

The Pope whistled convincingly.

'Your Holiness will doubtless recall . . .' began the Cardinal, but he was interrupted. 'Besides, the whole line from Rome to the port will be under the special protection of St Christopher, who as you know, or you ought to know, has taken over the job of patron saint of travel by rail. . . . Especially as We expect to use the line Ourselves frequently. We shall of course have Our own special train and carriages, like Queen Victoria, only on a grander scale. I envisage that

13

one carriage will be fitted up as a *carrozza-cappella*, so that We can pray as the Holy Spirit takes Us, and thus have a special facility to invoke blessed St Christopher in any emergency. The journey will take about two hours compared with the present five or six. It took Oudinot much longer than that, but military logistics . . .'

'Of course, Holiness. The convenience will be . . .'

'Not that We know anything about military matters,' said the Pope slyly. 'As you know We take care not to know. We are the Pope of peace, serving the Prince of Peace in this war-torn and disastrous nineteenth century. We have never raised our hand against any man. We have suffered humiliation and pain like our Blessed Saviour. What was meet for our revered predecessor Julius II is not in these days of unchivalrous weaponry for Us – and by the way, how is my Syllabus of Modern Errors coming along? But this is not what I was telling you about.'

Pius IX gave his Secretary of State his famous smile of unexampled sweetness, which so often got him his own way in spite of the Secretary of State's advice, and, so to speak, resumed his place in the train. 'In the matter of the line to Frascati the difficulties are of a different order.'

The Pope's voice took on a sterner note. Almost minatory. 'There will have to be a tunnel. Oh yes! That is unavoidable. The highway gradients would be impossible for the steam locomotive. It will, of course, add excitement to the journey, but also to the cost.'

In spite of himself, the Cardinal was beguiled. 'The cost? Can the Holy See afford a tunnel? We are not as rich as the English, who, I am told, have actually achieved a tunnel. But even they came a terrible financial cropper about the time Your Holiness, by God's infinite grace and to our unspeakable good fortune, was elevated to the See of St Peter. Yes, I recall it was just before the thrones of Europe, including your own, were shaken by that explosion of revolutionary liberalism . . .'

'Yes, yes,' said His Holiness. 'No need to go into that. We

14

THE THIN END OF THE WEDGE.

DARING ATTEMPT TO BREAK INTO A CHURCH.

The Pope forces the door of the Church of England
to let Cardinal Wiseman in, in order to steal its
ancient liberties.

also read the financial columns. Put it in the Syllabus. The English, though they did not fall into the pit dug by liberalism – they were more or less in it already – survived the crash. As the Rothschilds survived it likewise. Which, my dear Cardinal, is precisely the point. Rothschild will lend Us the money to build these railways, which will not stop at Frascati, for a line has also to be built from Rome to Bologna, to link together in lanes of shining iron all the parts of St Peter's Patrimony. From the Mediterranean to the Adriatic. From sea to shining sea. A holy work.'

The Secretary of State blenched. 'Is that really necessary, Holiness? It may give people ideas. A day's outing, half-price excursion trains Bologna to Rome – I mean to say, with all respect, your holy predecessor . . . did after all pronounce railways sinful and not to be introduced into this holy land of . . .'

'And was an absolute fathead. *"Chemin de fer c'est chemin de l'enfer."* Indeed! What is not? Any invention or discovery from Galileo onwards and even before that disastrous fellow is a source of temptation to Catholics. Stick that in the Syllabus somewhere. Yes, it is necessary! Look at what the foreign press – that is, the English press – is saying about the papal states; and screaming for reform. That ghastly person Gladstone is in Naples at this moment and might be here any day. Well, I gave them reform in '47 and what did they do with it? Killed people by the thousand. So I'm not giving it to them a second time. I'm giving them Progress instead. Progress! That is what they really want. And what does Progress mean, Secretary of State? It means railways, and gas lighting in the streets. Constitutions? Offer them a choice between a constitution and gaslight and they'll go for gas every time. Put constitutions in the Syllabus of Modern Errors, my friend, but leave out railways and gas.'

'As ever, Your Holiness's reasoning is infallible,' cried Cardinal Antonelli, 'but is it practicable? It would mean driving a line of rail over, or under, the Apennine mountains! It would require a regular miracle . . .'

'Over and under, I dare say,' said the Pope, smiling. 'Nor will a miracle be required. What will be required is the services of the eminent English engineer, Signor Thomas Brassey, and a huge loan from Rothschilds. Just as we have no army but employ France and Austria to defend us, in a so-to-speak beautifully balanced equipoise, so in the same way the money we save by not buying expensive soldiers can be devoted to servicing the large loan Baron Rothschild will dispense for Us at reasonable interest to pay for Signor Brassey's ingenuity in piercing the Apennines for Us. Do you not see, my dear Giacomo, in all this another manifestation of the Divine Providence to preserve our Patrimony against the machinations of, among others, Victor Emmanuel of Savoy, so that the temporal power necessary to securing the spiritual independence of the Holy See is buttressed by the involvement of other, often rival, interests, including Jewish banks and Protestant heretics?'

His Holiness's eye was drawn back again to his strategic map and the Secretary of State saw a chance, at last, to get down to the business of the afternoon.

'And on that very point, I mean relations with the British,' said Antonelli hurriedly, 'Your Holiness has waiting outside for an audience your newly created Cardinal Archbishop of Westminster, Monsignor Wiseman, who takes his leave of us before issuing his first pastoral message to his delighted flock, and then leaves for Vienna to have his audience with your faithful son and protector, Franz Josef, Emperor of Austria. The Chamberlain, Monsignor Talbot, is with him.'

'We've agreed to that, have We?' said His Holiness. 'We've been seeing an awful lot of the man lately. Such eyebrows! They put me off. However, if it's really the last time ... send him in ... though frankly, Giacomo, when it comes to the English, I'd rather be seeing Signor Brassey, in whose capacity to deliver I somehow feel greater confidence. Wiseman is enormously clever and is going to put all England at my feet, as you know. I only hope those benighted heretics won't find him too clever by half. Ah, my dear Cardinal Archbishop,

We are delighted to see you off on your great mission, with our blessing. You leave tomorrow?'

Cardinal Archbishop Wiseman got up from his knees and towered over the two Italians, and even over the English Chamberlain. 'Your Holiness, I thought before I publish my first Pastoral Letter to the English Catholics and tell them what felicity awaits them, you might like me to read it to you. It is addressed not only to them, but to all my fellow-countrymen, since I am announcing a new age, proclaiming a new epoch in their unhappy history. They are ready for it, as their so-called Church splits and fragments in every direction. It's called "Out of the Flaminian Gate" . . .'

'We shall read it, and their enthusiastic reception of it, in Italian, or Latin in due course,' said His Holiness. 'We shall, incidentally, be glad of a considerable increase in their voluntary contributions which their famous middle class can well afford. But just now We are rather busy with something else. So, dear and beloved Cardinal Archbishop, with our blessing, you are given leave to withdraw. . . .'

2

Mr John Thaddeus Delane took his seat in the London train shortly after lunch in Sandgate. That weekend he had tried to forget the paper and its problems. Not that it had many problems at the moment with an eight-page daily supplement of advertisements, and a waiting-list for insertions, a lead in circulation over all rivals put together, the latest printing machinery (to be displayed to the wonder of the public if this scheme of HRH for an international exhibition to celebrate world peace in a glasshouse in Hyde Park next year did not come to grief) and the finest news-gathering service in the world.

But it had turned nippy that October, he needed the foot-warmer as the carriage window admitted a slight draught, which perhaps accounted for his sense of unease. Yet the fact remained: *The Times* needed a new cause.

Indeed the fact was that he had not fully recovered his equanimity since his set-down by the pestiferous Palmerston. He had had to make it up with him after the July speech. *Civis Romanus Sum!* That mighty peroration still echoed three months on. Parliament had been converted almost to a man and the public had roared its approval; England held her head higher for that meretricious victory. He had turned the leader over to Henry Reeve on the morning after; a tart little piece, but it didn't get the editor off the hook. Secretly he had preferred *Punch*'s retort: 'Why don't you hit a man your own size?' Greece and *The Times* defeated, nay crushed, by mighty Britain and her fleet: what a glorious victory! As if it were Trafalgar come again! He remembered what the Prince had said to him that summer about the British public's ungovernable vulgarity, and (in the privacy of the palace) he had sadly agreed.

For it was no business of his to despise the almighty public, good gracious! That way lay the ruin of *The Times*! Rather, he had to lead the public in some righteous crusade! That way lay popularity and circulation. Triumphantly first with the news and omnisciently right with the views! That was the editor's proper stance, not truckling to a coxcomb of a minister. But truckled he had. And the worst was, everyone had been told about it. His dear two-faced friend and indispensable contact, that incorrigible gossip Charles Greville, had seen to that. And Lady Pam, of course. It was lucky that the end of the season had supervened so conveniently soon after the débâcle.

His titled acquaintance had seen him less frequently at the hunt that autumn.

All the same, he needed a campaign to hold his head as high in the drawing-rooms as it ought to be, used to be. Something justly to bring down his condign thunder. But what – what?

Of course they would go on with the Danish war, but the

19

complexities of Slesvig and Holstein now bored everyone, probably even Palmerston; if only he could warn of it as a cloud on the horizon threatening war with France and Austria like last summer – aha! But who cared about Prussia, or even Hanover, except the Royals? Chartism? That was all over, whatever Carlyle wrote in his maledictory *Latter-Day Pamphlets*.

The train groaned to a halt at London Bridge, where Mr Delane found his usual cabby ready to carry him to Serjeants Inn and his waiting correspondence.

And there it was!

Someone had told him that the Revd Dr Worldly Wiseman was returning to Rome and might be made a cardinal. He had thought at the time he might be a replacement for Lord Acton – a good thing as far as it went, perhaps. But this! A Cardinal Archbishop of Westminster! The cool appropriation of the City of Westminster, seat of the court and parliament of England, by a foreign priest and potentate: the plain theft of the time-honoured name most identified with the glories of our history and the very tombs of our kings and statesmen. To be renamed a Romanist see, reversing and repudiating the Reformation!

Oho! A defiant insulting of the Queen as the Supreme Governor of the Church of England. A spitting in the face of the English martyrs and a public rehabilitation of bloody Queen Mary . . . probably also of the Stuart line as the rightful monarchy of the realm. . . ! To what lengths of execration would Rome not go? Heavens, what an expression of supreme contempt for . . . for . . . well, for centuries of British history and liberty – and, ahem, what a gift to the press patriotically upholding that liberty. . . .

It was not to be borne!

The Times would not bear it.

The Times would rouse public opinion to refuse to bear it.

But wait. There must be more to come. The first despatch was brief. A mere summary from Paris. The full details of the bull had yet to come. And where was Wiseman? He had yet to say his say . . . *The Times* would proceed with due caution, first demolishing the cringing papal court sitting on French bayonets, and its impertinence, and – yes – lambasting the Puseys and their Tractarian acolytes who clearly had prepared for the coup and encouraged Rome to think it could get away with such an act of barefaced aggression. . . .

Ah yes, and that would please the Walter family, which was trying to live down its former tinkering with the Oxford Tractarian Movement, until its eyes were opened to the danger by the flow of conversions to Rome – notably Dr John Henry Newman – which was the inevitable consequence of these new papistical rituals and dogmas.

Yes, the preparatory barrage on every breakfast table tomorrow . . . but *suaviter in modo, fortiter in re.*

Henry Reeve would write it, and the Revd Thomas Mozley would follow it up next week, or possibly the Revd Henry Annersley Woodham, to engage the enemy's theological batteries; while Robert Lowe might be asked to ginger up Lord John Russell and the Cabinet to take the necessary political steps. . . . He was ready, now, to offer Lowe a permanent leader-writer position with *The Times.* If only Parliament were sitting! But probably that was why Rome had moved so fast after Pio Nono emerged from skulking in Naples when the French captured Rome from Mazzini for him. The plot was fast unfolding.

The story would run and run.

At ten he was entering Printing House Square, unsmiling, resolute. He nodded to his understrapper Dasent (who must know the news already), and sent for Reeve at once; he must give him the line personally, the usual handwritten note would not do. Dasent nodded understandingly; this was big, very big. Reeve, too, was ready, had been getting up the background since seven. The leader to be ready for submission to the editorial quill by midnight. Yes, yes, of course: *suaviter in modo, fortiter in re . . .*

'In a solemn consistery held at Rome on 30th September cardinals' hats were conferred on not less than fourteen new members of the sacred college. Among the causes of weakness and corruption by which the Church and Court of Rome have most suffered for centuries, and by which they have been reduced to their present helpless and dependent condition, one of the most fatal has been the purely Italian character of the governing body . . .'

Take that, Your Holiness!

'. . . Dr Wiseman has now been raised to the purple . . . we may regret that a deplorable perversion of religious opinion should have the effect of alienating a respectable Englishman [NB Irish, educated in Spain, Reeves marginalised] from the Church of his country and clothing him with the paltry honours of an Italian court. But England asks no divided allegiance, recognises no foreign honours, civil or military, without the express permission of her sovereign . . .'

Take that, Your Eminence!

'He is an English subject who has entered the service of a foreign power and accepts its spurious dignities . . .'

And that!

'The elevation of Dr Wiseman to the imaginary Archbishopric of Westminster signifies no more than to confer on the editor of *The Tablet* the rank and title of Duke of Smithfield . . .'

And that, Your Eminence and Your Holiness!

'It is the greatest act of folly and injustice which the Court of Rome has perpetrated since the Crown and people of England threw off its yoke . . . its only meaning is to insult the Church and Crown of England . . .'

(Which, though we refrain at the moment from underlining it, sounds a bit like a *casus belli* . . . and now for you Oxfordian turncoats):

'If there is one class of Englishmen more than another who ought to be sensitive to this vindication of the underlying pretensions of Roman authority it is precisely that class which most highly venerates the traditions and liberties of the English Church. They have mistaken our tolerance for indifference to their designs, and mistaken the renovated zeal of the Church for a return to Romish bondage, but we are not sorry their indiscretion has led them to show the power Rome would exert if it could by an act which the laws of this country will never recognise and which the public will deride when His Eminence the titular Archbishop of Westminster thinks fit to enter his diocese . . .'

In short, let the indignant populace throw bricks at him.

*   *   *

As Mr Delane was admiring the sunrise on his way home to bed, messengers were delivering the first parcels of copies to the General Post Office and to the new railway terminals; as the light advanced copies still wet from the presses were plumping through letter-boxes in Belgravia and Mayfair (to be ironed dry by butlers for adding to breakfast-tables and trays by the hundred); other batches were reaching stationers' shops throughout the metropolis. By mid-morning the news was whistling and steaming into provincial cities and cathedral closes; by afternoon it was fanning out by coach or van to rectories and vicarages, castles and country houses beyond the railheads; by midnight Edinburgh and Glasgow, wild Wales and rural Devonshire were receiving it just as another working day had begun in Printing House Square – and dozens of local newspapers were reprinting it verbatim for people who did not take in *The Times* but needed to be informed of its authoritative pronouncements.

From the statesman in his morning-room, the bishop in his study, the merchant in his counting-house to the man on the Clapham omnibus the Word had gone forth, and the Word was of *The Times*, so the Word was the truth, whose significance had been weighed by *The Times*; and behold it was clear to all from the tone of *The Times* that there was Trouble in the offing.

A stir rippled through the nation, a stir compounded of questioning voices, incredulous expostulations, preliminary denunciations, off-the-cuff judgements: a still puzzled but growing sense of outrage, as if the household cat had suddenly sprung up from the fireplace and bitten one savagely in the seat of one's trousers.

But the Athenaeum was still not fully afire, the Reform as yet only smouldering; the weeklies needed a few days to print, *The Illustrated London News* probably had not got a cut of His Holiness or even of the Vatican in stock: Delane knew the bellows must be judiciously applied to fan the flame into a conflagration. Here was a papal bid, he now added, to assert an authority that had never existed even before the Reformation! (And which even modern Catholic states kept under tight control.) Kings like Richard II had resisted it; the Statute of Praemunire, 1392, was still on the statute book unrepealed and forbidding the bringing of unauthorised papal bulls into the realm. English Catholics had themselves not asked for it, well satisfied in the liberties granted them by law in 1829 and governed by vicars-general for three hundred years. It was all the work of the Oxford renegades from the national Church who were plotting to restore a foreign usurpation over a consensus of men and women happy with the Bible and Prayer Book: plotting to sow division in our political society by an undisguised and systematic hostility to the institutions which were identified with our freedom and our faith; he (or rather the Revd Henry Annnersley Woodham, posting the leader from Jesus College, Cambridge) quoted the law as it stood, if so far unenforced: 'No foreign potentate hath any jurisdiction, power, superiority, pre-eminence or authority, ecclesiastical or spiritual, in this realm . . .'

Over to public opinion and the Government.

3

They were gathered in an upper room in the Shakespeare's Head in Wych Street discussing cartoons for the coming week over roast beef and Yorkshire pudding. It was quite a full attendance – Mark Lemon, Douglas Jerrold, Dicky Doyle,

Tom Taylor, Gilbert à Becket, the artists 'Phiz' Leech and Percival Leigh, Thackeray, who was shouting for another Double-X, Henry Mayhew, the social investigator on the *Morning Chronicle*, emerging from his Barclay Perkins, and the rest deep in sherry, 'off or on'.

'Well, what are we to do this week?' remarked Mark Lemon from the editorial chair in order to get ideas flowing. 'Another crack at this exhibition idea of the Prince's?'

'Too soon,' said Leech, who had been drawing on the table-cloth. 'We need to know a bit more about this feller Paxton and his glasshouse – people are taking to it, and our dear Colonel Sibthorpe's usual horror stories about anything new or progressive have only begun to circulate. Let's see the drawings which the Prince is putting on show and then call it something snide that will stick to it – like the "Crystal Palace", eh?'

'It's a damned dull week,' said Gilbert.

'What about a go at these Pre-Raphaelites?' said Taylor. 'I was talking to Coventry Patmore the other day and he says they are wildly excited about an absolute stunner of a girl from a milliner's shop who has agreed to float down the river for that dauber Millais to paint as Ophelia. Or something like that. It's the new realism. Remember how Millais disgusted everyone with his picture of Christ as a boy in his father's carpenter's shop this summer at the Academy? No haloes, and he used a street-urchin for his Christ. Dickens said so. And an Italian chap called Rossetti did an Annunciation that horrified everybody. Could we make something comic out of the "new realism"?'

'Going too far,' said Dicky Doyle.

'I could find them some realler realism to paint if they really want to shock the Academy – half-naked starving children sleeping rough in the doorways of the richest city in the world,' said Mayhew bitterly.

'But not for *Punch*,' said Lemon. 'We've done our bit with Tom Hood's "Song of the Shirt". Keep the rest of your shock-horror revelations for the *Morning Chronicle*, my dear fellows. We're supposed to show the funny side of life.'

'Ah, these indigent but complacent little milliners – what would young men too poor to get married do without them?' said Jerrold with a sly grin.

'Have you heard the one about the milliner and the bishop?' began Thackeray.

'Now now, order!' said Lemon. 'What about this craze for mesmerism and table-turning? I heard the nobility and gentry are taking it up. Mrs Carlyle has tried it and says it's a fraud. So has Browning.'

'How would we do it?' asked Jerrold.

'Ask this Dr Ashburner to demonstrate,' said Lemon.

The others did not seem enthusiastic.

'I believe there's something in it, as a medical technique,' said Thackeray, twisting his legs round a chair to ease a twinge of discomfort. 'I don't know this Dr Ashburner, but I do know a medical man who is certainly not a quack who uses it. . . . Let's not jump in too quickly before we make fun of it – I'll let you know more about it next week. But I say, what about this thing *The Times* is on about – making Dr Wiseman Cardinal Archbishop of Westminster? Delane is really stewed up about it, saw him at Lady Palmerston's last night, saying he was getting news of the Pope cutting England up into Catholic dioceses . . .'

'Don't like mixing with religion, unless it's political,' said Lemon, noticing that Dicky Doyle was frowning.

'Thought we *liked* the Pope,' said Leigh. 'Didn't I do a double spread of him as the only liberal sovereign in Europe, keeping his crown when all the rest were having theirs torn off by their oppressed subjects . . .'

'That was in '48,' said Thackeray. 'He's not a liberal now. He's using the Tractarian lot as a wedge to split the Church in half, convert the Romanist half to Rome, and turn 'em into an army of missionaries to dragoon the rest of us into obedience. Or so the Bishop of Oxford was telling friends of mine.'

'What? Soapy Sam?' queried Tom Taylor.

THE GUY FAWKES OF 1850

PREPARING TO BLOW UP ALL ENGLAND!

The Pope piles up the new Catholic bishoprics as fuel
with which to blow up parliamentary liberty and
Britain on Guy Fawkes' Day.

'That's him, charming feller to talk to,' said Thackeray, uncoiling and recoiling his legs.

'Where did you meet him?' asked Tom Taylor.

'At Lady Ashburton's. Delane was there too, the snake, going from one to another – you know his way: I am the great I am – so tell me all! And I will check what you say with Lord Aberdeen later! I expect Sammy got the story from him . . . a few minutes before he passed it on to the others.'

'You devious old tuft-hunter! I saw in the *Morning Post* that you were at Bath House on Tuesday. Anyway, let's see what *The Times* says. Julia! Got a copy of *The Times* downstairs? Lend it to us for a few minutes, will you? And another round of what we're having.'

'Sorry, sir. Gemman's got *The Times*, sir.'

'Well, who is this Wiseman?' asked Taylor, gulping sherry.

'Oh, I've met him somewhere,' said Thackeray. 'They say he's a bit like me. You know – big, beefy, bonhomous, untidy, tobacco all over his soutane, with a jolly laugh and a fund of totally unsmutty jokes . . .'

'Not like you, then,' snapped Lemon.

'The face of a sneaky villain, a spy, probably a Jesuit,' said Leech, scribbling busily and looking up at Thackeray now and then.

'Half Spanish, brought up in that branch of the Church Militant, conceived a great ambition, to convert England to the true faith, ran a sort of missionary training centre at Oxford, and saw the Tractarian Movement as the beginning of the process, so I'm told,' Thackeray said. 'His idea is to finish the job the abominable Pusey started with his Tracts against the establishment. Very natural, when you come to think of it. Went on with the good work in Rome, but I suppose things were slowed down when Mazzini's camarilla drove him out of Rome with the Pope. But he's now a cardinal with a red hat and all. I got most of this story from Monckton Milnes who knows Wiseman, of course! Says Wiseman – who nearly converted Milnes, believe it or not –

has organised the whole thing. Says his Roman friends have been calling him 'Your Eminence' as a joke for years. Said he was having a cardinal's coach built for him in Rome which will be grander than any of our bishops', even more splendid than the Lord Mayor's.'

'Oh, I say,' said Leech, 'I can use that!'

'Hold hard,' said Lemon. 'This is not next week's story – not yet...'

'But it will be,' said Tom Taylor. 'Why, it's a fund of copy if Thack has got it right. His Eminence Wiseman! The Pope's inquisitor! That's a man means ignorance, that's a man means priest-worship, that's a man means assumption of divine power by one man in a soutane over another in a mere frock-coat, powers to curse and bless, to deny or grant hope and heaven, powers to separate man, wife and child – powers to enter a statesman's cabinet or a queen's bedroom, powers there-fore to rule a kingdom...'

'Seen Macready's *Richelieu* at Drury Lane, have you, then?' chuckled Leigh. 'Why ain't he here tonight?'

'It sounds good,' said Lemon.' But let's get the facts, the full facts, before we go off half cock, as the Duke said to the pheasant... Julia! Is *The Times* free now? And the pens and paper...'

'*Times* is taken by another gemman, sir,' said their serving-maid, handing round the drinks 'And there's another gemman waiting for it, when he's finished. Tetchy he is, too. Been a run on it all day – is it a war or summat, sir?'

'Never mind,' said Lemon. 'We'll wait for it. Your health, Gentlemen!'

*   *   *

Now he had it all. Letters were flowing in. A few were de-fending the 'purely spiritual supremacy' that the papacy needed to organise, and which they averred no more af-fected the temporal sovereignty that the Queen exercised

29

over her subjects, Catholic and non-Catholic (English and Irish) alike. Not so, he and others thundered (or rather Robert Lowe thundered), for:

'Until we saw the whole scheme in black and white we were incredulous of the extent of its impudence: . . . the creation of twelve bishoprics, the systematic division of this island into a new fiefdom of Pope Pius IX . . . an audacious display of his intention to resume the absolute spiritual dominion of this island which Rome has never abandoned, but which, by the blessings of providence and will of the English people, she shall never accomplish. Never since the Reformation has the Court of Rome denied the validity of Anglican orders . . . the step now taken is one the Pope could not take in any other civilised country in Europe. . . .'

For the Pope had to ask the Austrian Emperor if he could install a particular prelate in any Austrian locality just as (*The Times* went on) when Canterbury had appointed an Anglican bishop in Jerusalem the Sublime Porte was asked for and had given its gracious legal permission first. . . . That was the protocol and only in tolerant England had the Pope dared to take advantage of our liberality to ride roughshod over it.

There was nothing to be feared from England, exulted the Cardinal in his triumphant pastoral, which, responding to the English papists in Rome for their grovelling congratulations, reassured his English flock and informed the chancelleries of Europe; he ordered that it should be read in all Romanist churches and chapels in England. For had not Lord Minto, the Prime Minister's father-in-law, agreed to an English hierarchy during his diplomatic visit to Rome before the revolutions in Europe had postponed its installation, which (it now transpired) had been urged upon the Pope by no less an adviser on English affairs than Father Nicholas Wiseman, Superior of the English College in Rome? All that remained to be done was for Lord John Russell to honour his father-in-law's word without ado.

The policy of Pius IX is (*The Times* summed it up) to trample on the rights of every national church and to concentrate the dominion of the whole of the Roman Catholic Church in its own ministers and emissaries, noting that Rome had now expressly ruled that all the privileges and customs of the Roman Church in England 'are abolished whatever their antiquity, and the new bishops are invested with full episcopal powers'.

These were the words of war, the demand for unconditional surrender. Thus were the conflicts of the seventeenth century resumed; this was how centuries of tolerance and peace were swept away.

The question was, what would the Government do about it?

4

Mr Charles Richards, senior secretary to the Board of Admiralty, by the grace of somebody who knew somebody to whom Lord Minto owed a small favour some years back, put his head round the door of the junior secretary (by the grace of Somebody Else High Up in Whig Arrangements), Thomas Carter, who was just hanging up his umbrella, and said, 'A private word with you, Mr Carter, if you please, before we have any meetings today. Come to my room, will you, without telling anyone.' And when Mr Carter was sitting facing him Mr Richards went on: 'Put everything on one side for the next few days. We are discussing war, and must be ready with at least an outline plan of operations to place before Sir Francis Baring personally, so he'll be fully briefed when he talks to Lord Palmerston.'

'War with whom – the French? I had not. . . . '

Nor had he; for days he had been busy with a little lady from the educational theatre representation in *poses plastiques* of the classical (not to say pagan) scenes taken from that year's Royal Academy Exhibition while his wife was having her ninth child.

'With France? No. With the Pope, of course. He's planning

to take over England. Haven't you been reading *The Times?*'

'War with *the Pope*,' gasped Mr Carter. 'How may battalions has the Pope got?'

'None, of course, nor warships either. Any more than Greece had in the summer. It's a matter of another blockade, as I see it. Civita Vecchia and Ancona – just as we blockaded the Piraeus until King Otho gave in. Admiral Sir William Parker sewed up Greece, and he can sew up the Pope the same way. All we have to do is to make a list of the ships and the stores we shall need and calculate the times they must be on station. I have been working on this. In Malta we have the flagship *Caledonia*, 120 guns, *Prince Regent*, 92, *Powerful*, 84, *Bellerophon*, 78, *Vengeance*, 84. Steamers, we have five screw sloops and ten or eleven paddlers, and . . .'

Mr Carter nodded. 'A tremendous squadron. But don't forget, sir, the coal question. Malta is, let's see, three hundred miles from Civita Vecchia. And winter is drawing in . . .'

'When His Holiness sees our big ships standing off his coast he'll think again about cutting us up into Catholic dioceses!'

'Yeees, he might. Unless France decides she must support Oudinot in Rome when his supplies are cut off. Her fleet in Toulon might be greater than our strength . . .'

'Which simply means reinforcements from the home ports. We've got the ships, Carter, we've got the men, we've got the money too.'

'True, sir. But unfortunately the ships at home are, as you know, mostly sailing-ships and by now unseaworthy, or are clapped-out paddle-steamers that can hardly make five knots – especially in winter weather – while the French are building nothing but screws . . .'

'I wish you wouldn't go on about screw ships, Carter. It's a fallacious argument to say we should build more. Paddle-steamers are ideal for getting our capital ships into action, whatever the wind or weather. One on either beam towing them into position. Then the hundred-gun broadsides – *Crash!* Your big steamer carries twenty or thirty guns. Admiral Parker always doubted the utility of screw ships, except as scouts. Bah! The French won't face a hundred-gun first-rate towed into action by two powerful paddle-steamers.'

'But the French are building big steamers clad with thick iron armour . . .'

'Which will then sink. Don't be a ninny, Carter . . .'

'And our spies have wind of a plan to use dozens of steamers to land thirty thousand infantry and cavalry on our shores overnight . . .'

'That's an old wives' tale, and we don't pay spies to make it up! We have no spies in Brest or Toulon, Carter, and we don't need any. They are ungentlemanly. We are not afraid of war in France. And let me tell you this: if there *was* war with the Pope and France, the Romans would rise *en masse* and chuck the Pope and Oudinot out, neck and crop, under *Caledonia*'s guns!'

'Really, sir? How do you know that?'

'We have our intelligence agents in the Holy City, Carter. This nice young Mr Hallam is one. Now let's draw up my plan for Sir Francis Baring, and we'll see what Pam – that is, the Foreign Secretary – thinks of it. And do read what *The Times* says, especially between the lines.'

*   *   *

'Well, what did Pam say, dear?'

Enveloped in a vast padded peignoir, Lady Russell had intruded on her spouse's breakfast, kissing him with a conjugal kiss after he had daintily wiped his mouth of the faintest trace of boiled egg stains. He was a neat little man and he loved her devotedly.

She loved him too, in spite of his littleness. But she was always alert for any opportunity to make him seem a little less little. It was a triumph, of course, that he was prime minister; but that a very small stature and an inability to raise his voice involved a lurking risk of ridicule to a prime minister was always obvious to her. Her husband did not always dominate, even in Cabinet; the House was a permanent headache. Sometimes, as she watched his performance at the despatch-box from the peeresses' gallery she found her handkerchief soaked in – perspiration. He was at his best when he had something weighty to explain such as reforming the franchise; or when the House was totally with him anyway, for example in shouting down Lord Ashley's ruinous factory bills to reduce working hours to ten a day, six days a week. But latterly the House was not usually with him. Latterly it was with Pam, who (admittedly) had such a wonderful voice.

'Pam wasn't keen on the war idea.'

'Oh, indeed! Was that what kept you at Carlton House Terrace so late last night? Trying to persuade him that wherever a British subject is wronged, the strong arm of England will be outstretched to protect him. Haven't we all been wronged by the Pope appropriating Westminster, especially the Queen? Westminster isn't very far to stretch one's arm, surely?'

'No, but Rome apparently is. He says it is a war we can't win, and one the Pope would win, in fact one that the Pope, if he has any sense, will positively invite.'

'I thought he had.'

'Pam says it'd be a war we can't fight and he isn't going to pick up the papal glove. He isn't even going to bluster. Said I must get out of my own mess this time...'

'Why can't we fight it? We've got the ships, we've got the men...'

'Pam pointed out to me that half the ships are unseaworthy, and even if they weren't we have no cordage in stock to rig them and no gunpowder for their guns – and that even if we had, half the men are Irish Roman Catholics who would refuse to fight the Pope, and that would be a signal for the French and the Austrians to declare a holy war on us, while our own Catholics would embrace the chance of becoming martyrs for the Faith, especially the new Puseyite converts. Especially Dr Newman. Pam says we're beat before

34

we fire a shot. Asked me who put this silly idea about. It wasn't me, anyway. It was Lord Winchilsea, I think, or one of his fanatics.'

'Yet everybody hates the Pope. Mrs Brookfield told me that young Henry Hallam, who has just been in Rome, says in his last letter that the Romans would rise against the papal government if they had half a chance. And Mr Gladstone says . . .'

'I know. "The negation of Christianity erected into a system of government." Pam knew about it. But he says it's no go, all the same.'

'Then what are you going to do, darling?'

'I don't know yet, I'm thinking about it.'

'You must do something. *The Times* says so. The country is seething. It looks to you for a decisive lead, my love.'

'I know, my love. I'm giving it careful thought. At least I can tell the Queen that I stopped Pam from involving us in a disastrous war.'

'Pam will tell them that *he* stopped *you.*'

'They'll believe me, not Pam. They think he is bent on getting us hated by every government in Europe. You know that, dear. You've told them so yourself.'

'I hardly needed to, my sweet! But you're prime minister. You've got to do something. Call the Cabinet, for instance.'

'The Cabinet is shooting grouse, thank the Lord. It is not available for consultation. I must act on my own initiative. I am prime minister.'

'But what are you going to *do*, in heaven's name, John?'

'I am thinking about it, my dear. I won't let His Holiness get away with this, you may be sure. He has insulted the Queen.'

'How insulted does Her Majesty feel, John, do you know?'

'Not quite as much as I could wish. I'm told she went about shouting "Am I Queen or am I not?" for a few hours, but then cooled off. I may have to talk to the Archbishop of Canterbury.'

'Sumner? Don't waste your time, dear.'

5

It was the great age of breakfasts. Your friends came to your rooms between ten and eleven where a substantial repast awaited them: joints, pies, fish, puddings, toast and marmalade, tea, coffee, sherry and white wines – and, above all talk and tobacco. You talked and tucked in until four or five, when the party broke up to enable people to stagger home to dress for dinner and the round of evening parties, mostly given by the great Whig hostesses, but many by less exalted members of society – even at times by great and famous artists like Landseer.

The giver of the best breakfasts, it was commonly agreed, was Mr Monckton Milnes, MP, in his fine bow-windowed apartments in Pall Mall. Mr Milnes knew everybody; but if he didn't happen to have met a desirable guest for breakfast, he invited him (or on occasion her) just the same. Few refused. It was also widely known that it gave Mr Milnes particular pleasure to invite people who did not see eye to eye on political, social or literary matters to the same breakfast party. The resulting contention supplied him with additional anecdotes to add to his large and entertaining stock. He had had Mr Disraeli and Mr Cobden to the same breakfast! He was happy, moreover, to be the hero or the dupe of the stories going the rounds; he was delighted to have appeared recognisably if unfavourably in one of Mr Disraeli's novels, and the fact that he had crossed the floor from the Tory benches to the Whigs (and resigned from the Carlton Club) helped keep him at the centre of gossip. Wagers were currently laid on his converting to fashionable Romish Puseydom, but there were much larger bets on the possibility that he would shortly convert from bachelordom to matrimony. Among the *on dits* was the fact that Miss Florence Nightingale was back in England: had they met again? And so on.

Mr Milnes was thinking that today's party had been a

success. Bishop Wilberforce had graced the occasion and even said grace; the Carlyles had come and Carlyle disliked the Bishop, and his wife Jane had sniffed loudly during grace; the Bishop in his turn reprehended the tone of the Sage's recent pamphlets pouring contempt on the gross inefficiency of the governing clique and lauding the late Sir Robert Peel to the skies. The Brookfields had come, ever scenting preferment: so Thackeray had also come and made his usual discreet but helpless sheep's eyes at the lovely Jane Brookfield. This platonic passion had gone on for years, but he had not written a novel about it. Mr G.H. Lewes, a journalist on that free-thinking periodical, *The Leader*, had come; its freely expressed criticisms of monogamy and championship of the rights of women reflected his personal experiences in a remarkable matrimonial threesome which could only jar on the Bishop, the Carlyles and the Brookfield–Thackeray triangle. Furthermore a remarkable young lady, Miss Mary Ann Evans, had accepted his invitation also: her notorious translation of Herr Professor Strauss's *Das Lebens Jesus* must be even more upsetting for a bishop than the indecorous freedom in which she lived in the household of her publisher Mr Chapman; yet the unexceptionable Mr Herbert Spencer had escorted her, despite the well-known fact that he considered Mr Carlyle a fatuous windbag. It was immediately plain that Mr Lewes was impressed by her and she by him. Yet everybody said that she was going to marry Spencer, since Mr Chapman was already married. At the last minute, moreover, Milnes had roped in two more guests: one was the Revd Charles Kingsley, the avowed Chartist, known as 'Parson Lot', whose best-selling novel *Yeast* was more Dickensian than *David Copperfield* – in fact it was barefaced socialist propaganda which had had editorial treatment by *The Times* – and who was there to buttonhole the Bishop and put the case for him to concert the support of all the other bishops for a massive campaign of slum clearance. A man, in short, who would stop at nothing. Finally there was the remarkable Dr Ashburner, who believed he could cure Carlyle's (and other people's) indigestion (and gout) by mesmerism.

A key element was missing: if only Cardinal Wiseman himself could have joined the party, thought Mr Milnes, and he said so aloud.

'But would he have come?' asked Mr Lewes.

'Oh yes. Known him for years. Saw him off when he went to Rome to get his hat. Of course he's a total anachronism, another Hildebrand. But he'd charm you, impress you, nearly convert you – had a go at me years back, and got me as far as turning Tractarian . . . for several weeks.'

The Bishop had chuckled in his worldly tone. The so-called Cardinal had not arrived in Britain yet, he told the company, and he really wondered when he would sneak in, for the revulsion shown by the public must have been a shock to him. Had they read his declaration to the Catholics in Britain? In case they would like to have a taste of its impudence, he had brought a copy with him; and duly amused them by reading some of it in a mock ecclesiastical voice '". . . the great work then is complete, what you have long desired and prayed for is granted. Your beloved country has received a place among the fair churches which form the splendid aggregate of the Catholic communion: Catholic England has been restored to its orbit in the ecclesiastical firmament from which its light had long vanished . . . um, yum. . . . How must the saints of our country look down from their seats of bliss upon this new evidence of the faith and church which led them to glory . . . um, yum . . . and all those blessed martyrs who have fought the battles of the Faith, who mourned, more than over their own fetters and their own pain, the desolate way of their own Sion and the departure of England's religious glory. . . ." In short,' said the Bishop, 'he has made a savage attack on the Anglican establishment as a total nullity. He has forbidden Roman Catholics to attend our services, even to enter our churches except perhaps as students of archaeology. . . .'

The Bishop choked on his words and resorted to another glass of sherry.

The Brookfields dutifully voiced incredulous disgust. 'My Lord, we must resist these abominations,' Mr Brookfield cried; but Mr Milnes was gratified by the ribald laughter and comments of the other guests: 'Back to the ages of faith and filth,' snorted Mrs Carlyle. 'It will keep *Punch* in copy for weeks,' said Thackeray enthusiastically, beginning to sketch on his host's damask table-cloth a sleeping John Bull having a cardinal's hat pressed on his brows by an evilly grinning triple-crowned pontiff. Miss Evans, looking appreciatively over his shoulder, remarked, 'Isn't it Guy Fawkes' Night next week? Perhaps he will learn something from our annual national celebration? Or will he do as Catholicism usually does, convert it into a hallowed Roman tradition and turn Fawkes into St Alban, who died to convert England from paganism?'

'He'll never get away with it,' said Mr Spencer plummily. 'Sociology and social evolution are taking modern man into a new age.' But the Revd Brookfield saved the Bishop's embarrassment by intoning, 'This is the harvest of tares that Pusey has sown in our innocent fields. He is the enemy that has done this. Draw him breaking into a church using a crozier as a jemmy, Thack my boy,' he added, using his napkin to mimic a masked burglar, who somehow looked clerical, and making them all chuckle.

'Alas, my dear friends,' said the Bishop, 'Mr Brookfield has hit the nail on the head. This has long been prepared by Pusey and his friends, though he denies it. Look at the harvest that has been already been taken by Rome. Only recently I had to require one of my clergy to resign his living when he refused to adhere to the Articles of the Church, insisting on the bodily presence, and refusing to give up his practice of hearing his lady parishioners' personal confessions in the rectory study, and advising them on the details of the amendment of their lives. Within a fortnight of my forbidding him to mount his pulpit he had gone over to Rome, from infidelity to the empire of infidelity! Only the latest in a long line of them. Alas,' – he lowered his voice – 'my own brother fell into the ambush. Oxford was the centre of the disease. But I can say I have never promoted a member of my clergy who proved to be infected.'

'Who creep and intrude and climb into the fold – Milton, *Areopagitica*,' said Brookfield, winning an approving nod from His Lordship.

'*Lycidas*,' said Mrs Carlyle and Miss Evans together.

'You're losing them by the score,' added Miss Evans. 'In an age of doubt the weak long for certainty, and Rome offers them more certainty than you do, Bishop – or even your science does, dear Mr Spencer. Rome is infallible, you can't match that, either of you! It is a licence to turn one's back on personal responsibility. One faith, one people, one pope. Think of the reverent Gorham, the English bishops all at sixes and sevens, the Privy Council called in to decide whether baptism purges an infant of original sin – or ... or if it doesn't, you know,' she said in comical bewilderment, and nearly everyone laughed.

'Only folly brought the Privy Council into it at all,' protested the Bishop. 'Purely spiritual questions, like the regeneration of infants, should be left to purely spiritual judges, and they could have been if the dispute had gone from the Court of Arches direct to the Archbishop of Canterbury – but Sumner is weak as water. Don't quote me on that,' he added to Thackeray, who nodded solemnly.

'But what does Gorham himself believe, My Lord?' asked Brookfield.

'Nobody knows what he believes,' sighed the Bishop. 'Certainly not the Privy Council. But whatever it is, his bishop, Exeter, still thinks it heretical and now that the Privy Council has given him back his living, which was Gorham's main object, refuses to have anything to do with him.'

Carlyle had been slowly getting up steam, as he puffed whorls of smoke from his churchwarden pipe up the chimney.

'Excommunicated by the Bishop of Exeter, but not by the Bishop of Oxford, eh,' he snarled. 'That sort of thing was common in the Middle Ages, and the Faith survived it. Survived three popes at once, for the matter of that. But it

40

THE POPE IN HIS CHAIR.

With Mr. Punch's Compliments to Lady Morgan.

Punch was full of skits based on a lady archaeologist's claim that she had seen an Arabic inscription on 'St Peter's chair', which clearly was looted by the Crusaders.

won't survive the way you are going on, or the Pope either. Because the Faith is dead under you both – dead, I say! And has been these two hundred years. Now we have a new philosophy, worship of mammon, the pig-philosophy which leaves capitalists' pockets full and the people's pockets empty – and both of them dying of inner emptiness and ennui in a world of fast trains and steamers, electric telegrams, and change and speed for the so-called better. Whatever is new, is better! The temples to the new religion are the railway terminals, and its cathedral is being built of glass in Hyde Park – glass a very suitable material for the worship of materialist progress! Breaks easily to let in the winds of disillusionment and of dissolution! The new! The latest fashion! The fastest engine! The exhilaration of going fast, fast never mind where! It is sufficient to be going fast, that is sufficient satisfaction! Instead of faith we now have the exhilaration of steam worship and phallus worship, and there is nothing else that is real. . . .'

The Bishop tried to say 'Ahem', and Kingsley and Thackeray were vainly trying to insert a word edgeways, while Mrs Carlyle put on an unfathomable expression, Miss Evans almost a roguish one; but Spencer knew the prophet only too well, and had turned away to the bow window with a shrug. Outside, the carriages, drays, vans, cabs, sandwichboardmen and police struggled in an inextricable tangle. All that was needed, Spencer decided, was a rule that everyone should keep to the left and the police should enforce it. But the Sage despised utilitarianism, and never looked out of windows.

'Leadership alone could do something for this age,' Carlyle thundered on. 'The leadership that Peel gave us over the corn imbroglio, but Peel is dead and there is no substitute. There was no substitute for Oliver Cromwell either. Where there is no vision, the people perish. *Laissez-faire* is neither a vision nor a law like those of the mighty Isaac Newton, and the Economisters like Bagehot point the way to ruin. So would my old friend John Stuart Mill, had he not met his guardian angel, Mrs Taylor, and now sees the truth, or some of it. What I see is men and women who have no work, and never will, and, as I have said, the Government might as well shoot them for all the use they have for them either here or in Ireland, when there is work a-plenty to be done draining the land and putting it into production from Galway to ... to ... to the Fens. And all that is needed to do it is to form our wretched paupers into disciplined companies of workers led by leaders with an iron resolution, like Oliver Cromwell and. . . .'

But the Sage now doubled up in pain, turned to his wife and gasped, 'My blue pills – quick!'

In a moment Dr Ashburner was at his side making passes over his writhing form. Either these or the pills administered by his wife seemed to bring relief, but for the moment he was silenced. 'Devilled kidneys,' said Thackeray compassionately. And suddenly the Prophet gave forth a sound as of a great trumpet and hurriedly rose up gasping, 'Excuse me, I must . . .', and his host rushed him from the room.

In the confusion only Charles Kingsley heard Spencer's comment: 'Oddly enough a pamphlet recently crossed my desk advocating exactly that policy. Armies of workers under trained and stern leadership. It is entitled *Das Kommunistiche Manifest* by somebody called Karl Marx.'

'You've got something like it already in the eastern counties,' said Kingsley. 'Capitalists form gangs of desperate unemployed labourers, of all ages and both sexes, which they hire out to farmers at starvation wages and make a nice profit out of it. They are indeed ruthless. Has Carlyle that sort of thing in mind? Excuse me, I must catch a quick word with the Bishop before he goes. . . .'

Yes, thought Mr Milnes, as his guests straggled forth, it had been an enjoyable breakfast. It had taken his mind off his anxieties. What were his chances with Annabel Crewe? He needed to get married. He was over forty. He was getting plumpish – no, be honest, fat. His political career had run into the sands. No hope of office under Lord John, even after three years of waiting since he had converted to Whiggery. Yet he was papabile, everyone said so. If only there were a ministry of culture – how well he would run it! No, he must settle down at last and Annabel would do; to be mistress of Fryston Hall would surely appeal. Everybody was getting married this year – even Tennyson! A pure woman to initiate: the conversion of absolute innocence into total experience – an agreeable procedure, he'd been given to understand.

And that reminded him, the bookseller Turner had written to say the book he wanted, with the engravings, had come in. There were books that everyone should read but didn't and books nobody should read, but did. '*The Wedding Night*, a voluptuous disclosure', offering 'methods of raising the animal spirits and reviving the drooping energies of age, &c.' seemed almost to fall into both categories! It deserved a place on the shelves of Fryston's *Aphrodisiopolis*. He'd time to visit Holywell Street and get back in time to dress for dinner: Rogers, Dickens, Maclise and also Tennyson, the new Poet Laureate, who was house-hunting as usual but also wanted to see if Mr Samuel Rogers's court dress would fit him for size. It had belonged to Wordsworth, and Rogers could have worn it if he had not refused the laureateship on the ground of age, thus making way for Tennyson. As things were, continuity would be preserved, if only sartorially. It promised to be a hilarious party.

6

'I hope I'm not interrupting you, dear,' said Lady Russell. 'It's just that I've got an idea for a way of dealing with the Pope.'

'Really, dear?' said the Prime Minister, looking up from his desk. 'Actually, I'm just drafting a letter in reply to one from old Maltby, the Bishop of Durham, you know. I'll read it to you. He wants me to define my attitude to the papal insults. I think my reply gives a lead to the nation. . . . But

I see you are bursting with your idea. Let us hear it first.'

Lady Russell perched on the edge of her husband's desk, hitching up her crinoline. 'Harriet called – you know, Lady Ashburton. I know you find her tiresome, but she does see everybody.'

'I find her very tiresome and catty, and keep my distance as much as possible.'

'Yes, well. The point is she has been talking to Mazzini, who's back in London. You know, Prime Minister, even if Pam says we can't go to war, we still might be able to create a diversion which would frighten the Pope and then, in exchange for our good offices, he would give up the hierarchy plan or at least postpone it. In diplomacy a plan postponed is often a plan shelved indefinitely.'

Lord John Russell's eyes narrowed. 'Mazzini? Well, go on.'

'Mazzini suggests we should give him some financial backing for fomenting a revolution in northern Italy. It's what the Pope fears most, and then, you see, we could. . . .'

The Prime Minister gazed at his wife with his frostiest expression. 'I beg you will forget that you ever even discussed this madman's ideas with Lady Ashburton. He has just tried to . . . er . . . foment a revolution in Milan and failed miserably. That's why he's back here, penniless again, to start more mischief no doubt. If he got funds from us, first, it would leak out and be seen as a hostile act by France and Austria, and secondly it wouldn't be a diversion, because if he had any success he'd go on to try and liberate Italy as he and Garibaldi tried to do in Rome, and forget about any interests we had. And if he succeeded, he'd make Italy a socialist republic. The man's a red, a radical, a revolutionist, a religious crank and – and a Chartist. I can't imagine why respectable people take him in and give him support. "Friends of Italy" they call themselves, forsooth! No, dearest, no, no, no! I am quite sure I speak for Pam on this. Pam refused to rescue him when the French squashed that Roman Republic of his. We were all sorry when he escaped. He is a threat to the upper classes everywhere. No! Italy is a geographical expression, like Germany, and no more. The only way it could be anything else is if a constitutional monarchy like ours could be established there as a United Kingdom of Italy. That won't happen for a century, if ever. Pam says so. Now let me read you my letter to Maltby. It will be published in *The Times* at once.'

The little man's sweet smile had broken through and he stroked his wife's hand to soften his summary obliteration of Mazzini. She was a wonderful helpmeet, but there was a limit, confined to the drawing-room, to what women could do in politics, and one had to put one's foot down occasionally. He picked up a sheet of paper.

'Listen: "There is an assumption of power in all the documents which have come from Rome, a pretension of supremacy over the realm of England and a claim to sole and undivided sway which is inconsistent with the Queen's supremacy, with the rights of our bishops and clergy, and with the spiritual independence of this nation as asserted even in Roman Catholic times ..."'

'But we know all that already.' There was a peevish note in Lady Russell's voice.

'"Even if it shall appear that the servants of the Pope have not transgressed the law I feel we are strong enough to resist any outward attacks ..."'

'But that's admitting defeat at the very start ...'

'Do wait, dear. "I will only say the law shall be carefully examined" – that's a warning to Rome! "There is a danger which alarms me much more than the aggression of some foreign power. Clergymen who have subscribed to the Thirty-nine Articles and acknowledged the Queen's supremacy have been most forward in leading their flocks to the very edge of the precipice. The honours paid to saints, the claim of infallibility of the Church, superstitious use of the sign of the cross, the recommendation of auricular confession ..." – that's where the priests and the Jesuits get their grip on the women and therefore the children, Fanny, the nation of the future. I go on: "... all these things are pointed out by clergymen of the Church of England as worthy of adoption . . ."'

'Pusey! Tractarian traitors. But we *know* that, dear. *The Times* said it days ago. Everybody has got the message.'

'I have put it a little more elegantly, dear. Listen: "I shall not bate a jot of heart or hope so long as the glorious principles of the Reformation shall be held in reverence by the great mass of the population which looks with contempt at the mummeries of superstition and with scorn at the laborious efforts which are now being made to confine the intellect and enslave the soul." There! That'll give them something to think about.'

'Well put, dear, well put. But what will it *do*?' Nettled, Lady Russell could not keep a touch of impatience out of her voice.

'As I said, examine the legal position.'

'But that won't frighten them! Your lawyers will take months. Now is the moment to strike before the Cardinal – Wiseman, I mean – actually enters the country in his gilded coach with his red hat on his head to hear plans are going ahead for his enthronement, which will make a coronation look like a village fête – at any rate to the Irish who are daily pouring in. I've seen them begging, even in Piccadilly. What are the police about? And the Roman priests are now wearing full clericals in the streets – yes, in Piccadilly and Whitehall, under your nose. Cassocks and clerical collars and shovel hats and rosaries swinging from their necks! *Punch* suggests you should bring in a bill making it a treasonable offence to assume a titular role without permission of the Queen, so that you can pack off Wiseman and his bishops to Botany Bay for life.'

'I do not take advice from a ribald radical rag! And the penalty for treason is not transportation, it's hanging and I can't . . .'

'At least they are suggesting doing *something* . . .'

'I shall be doing what I say in my letter. And by the way, my dear, I have received an impudent letter from Wiseman, who is in Brussels. It ought to interest you. You remember we sent your father on that fact-finding mission to Italy four years ago? Well, Wiseman claims that your father fully agreed, at a meeting with the Pope, to Rome installing a full-blown hierarchy here.'

'No! Papa couldn't possibly . . .'

'Wiseman says Lord Minto saw the Pope's proposals in Rome and raised no objection to them. So the Church assumed it could go ahead without further discussion. The delay was caused by Mazzini's seizure of Rome, which forced the Pope to take refuge in Naples. Well, of course, Minto should have reported the whole thing to me, but, my dear, frankly we know what he's like. He didn't know what he was doing half the time he was in Italy. He certainly never told me, or the Foreign Office, that he'd seen any such proposals. Your father has given us a headache. By neglecting to minute this incident, he has given them a case to argue against us. A bad case, but there need not have been a case at all. It's my fault for giving him the job, but I didn't think he could do any harm, he did so want to go, and it seemed nice for the family, but I'd have done better to have sent a professional diplomat.'

Lady Russell marched out of the room with a swish of skirts and drapery, saying, 'I shall give Father a talking-to, I can promise you that. From now on I shall not pass on any of his suggestions for jobs in the Civil Service for members of my family. I can promise you *that*, too.'

Lord John Russell added some further touches to his letter to the Bishop of Durham with priggish satisfaction.

7

England was on fire from end to end. In parks, in gardens, in backyards, flames and smoke billowed up to the muddy London sky; bouts of rain hissed ineffectually upon the conflagrations. On village greens, in open spaces in the small towns, and vying with the reflections of the blast-furnaces in manufacturing cities of the north, mighty pyres blazed and roared amid the shouts and cheers of citizens, young and old, who danced round, and fed, the fires. In the streets, not only of the capital but in such staid communities as Exeter and Ware, torchlight processions moved purposefully, leading tumbrils in which fettered victims bounced and nodded horribly, like penitents at *autos-da-fé*. Passengers in trains saw the flames as they whirled by, reminding those who were old enough of the widespread rick burnings of twenty years back when the agricultural labourers had impiously revolted after their request for sixpence extra on their weekly wages was refused by the farmers, and had to be put down by the yeomanry and dragoons. Incendiarism was abroad once again.

Here and there rockets soared into the sky, recalling Mr Congreve's remarkable military inventions, and, like his, frequently overcharged, exploded prematurely; the fiery projectiles of Roman candles shot upwards, Bengal lights, serpents and blazing wheels illuminated the scene and the incessant popping of firecrackers by small boys, not infrequently under ladies' skirts, resembled musketry, the shrieks of the affronted sounding like so many casualties. As the processions reached town squares, the city fathers awaited the demonstrators in ermine and gold braid, while brass bands blared out 'The British Grenadiers' and other martial tunes; as a column of fire rose perilously close to Exeter's ancient fane the mayor called for three cheers, whereupon the revellers uncovered and sang the national anthem right through, including with special gusto those verses which allude to the foreigner's knavish tricks and politics – twice over, for good measure.

These *autos-da-fé* had of course been in preparation for some days amid juvenile solicitations of 'a penny for the old guy', but were backed up this year by more open-handed munitions from certain of the gentry, including barrels of surplus tar; but Lord John's letter to the Bishop of Durham had been received with superadded fervour as a war-cry by all classes of a people whose blood was now most thoroughly up, and determined to make it hot for the 'mummeries of superstition'.

England was burning the Pope.

The figure in the tumbrils was no longer crowned with a battered topper as had been usual in the past; loving hands had got busy with cardboard, glue and tinsel, and the topper had been transfigured into the triple crown of the Roman aggressor; in the more ambitious celebrations something that aped pontifical robes pinned together the sacks of straw stuffed with small bags of gunpowder, which constituted his sacred body; while a second figure supposed to represent Cardinal Wiseman had been, here and there, seated behind the central figure, and made recognisable by a red hat, a form of head-gear which was also familiar to Protestant merry-makers.

In London, Mr Mazzini supplicated the crowd: 'Do you suppose,' he cried, 'that if the republican flag of Italy had still been floating over the Quirinale in Rome, Pope Pius IX would have dared attempt his aggression against England? No! The Pope is hated in Rome and in Italy. I cheer you noble English who resist his arrogance!'

The crowd responded with enthusiasm and cries of 'Good old Mazzy!'

The New Police, in top hats, politely kept order, extinguishing any unofficial subsidiary fires and dealing with those persons who (to the disgust of serious churchly protesters) had fortified themselves unduly heavily at alehouses on the way. They also stood guard, truncheons drawn, at any Catholic establishments that happened to stand along the line of march. Beside them, unarmed but prepared to show that muscular Christianity was no monopoly of Chartist preachers of the Word in the slums, stood groups of popish clerics, determined to defend the outward and visible signs of the superstitious mummeries denounced by Lord John.

For the rest, their newly converted parishioners stayed at home, while the so-called Old Catholics went out to their dinner parties, and to attend the opera and theatres, with the same genial disdain for such outbursts of religious ex-citement among their neighbours as they had put up with over the past three hundred years without a hierarchy to stir them to new witness for the Faith. Gazing at the scene they tended to regret the apostasy of the Duke of Norfolk, who in protest at the whole affair had attended a Church of England service the previous Sunday, but with a certain sympathy. They had for some time found the intrusions into their lives of a new and Romanising Irish and Italian imported priesthood very trying.

Many of them were Whigs and forgave Lord John's testiness on the plea that politics forced him to say something; others were Tory and noted that Wiseman's new heaven and earth in England were not likely to include any improvement in the depressed price of corn.

Peering from the windows of his lodgings in Dean Street, Soho, Herr Karl Marx said: 'What a people they could be, these English, if only they were properly trained and aimed at the right target! But anyhow if it's a boy, as I hope, I shall call him Guy Fawkes; *Jawohl!* Guy Fawkes Marx, my dear little revolutionist! What is it?' he cried as the nurse brought in the wrapped bundle for his inspection and the moans next door died away. 'A boy! A boy! Welcome to the world revolution, my darling son!'

The long-established and officially recognised hierarchy of Ireland tut-tutted at the barbaric spectacle across the sea, and concluded not without some satisfaction that Cardinal Wiseman would have his work cut out if he expected to extirpate heresy as swiftly as his Pastoral Letter 'Out of the Flaminian Gate' seemed to promise the trustful Holy Father.

Rain had quenched the last embers of the bonfires when His Eminence disembarked from the packet at Dover and blessed a very small gathering of kneeling parishioners. But even St Augustine had had to start in a modest way, he told himself, as he settled in his first-class carriage. He recalled that a consignment of twenty-one thousand crucifixes, and thousands of plaster statuettes of the Blessed Virgin, together with huge stocks of prints of sacred hearts and rosaries, had gone on ahead of him by steamer. That was the objective, something to live up to.

*   *   *

They were arguing fiercely round Millais's canvas. 'You see, I was right about the emerald green,' Holman Hunt was saying, 'and the poppy oil and copal resin medium gave him freedom to work in the open air without too much drying. It stays tough and flexible.' Dante Gabriel Rossetti shook his head and was about to protest when there came a loud knock at the door, and Mrs Millais, the artist's adoring mother, pulled in Mr Coventry Patmore with a gust of fog and rain from Gower Street.

Apologising for his sneeze as he accepted her help in divesting himself of his cape and muffler, the man known to the Brotherhood as 'Our Poet', a man who dined with Carlyle and Thackeray, followed her to the door of the studio (which she was forbidden to enter) and greeted them all with affection. He was noted for having an angel in his house for a wife and was known to be writing a long mystical poem about her connubial and housewifely virtues (which included the authorship of a published manual on the proper management of servants – though at the moment Mrs Patmore could afford but one thin skivvy).

'What!' cried Rossetti with fulsome disappointment. 'No heavenly Emily? Have you left your angelic soul at home? Is this but the soulless apparition of a beautiful young man we see before us, and who has avoided us for weeks?'

'No, it's a sodden assistant librarian at the British Museum, if you want the facts for once, brother Gabriel,' replied Patmore, with another sneeze, 'wearing a muffler the angel has knitted for me. Hail Stephens, my dear boy! And our didactic Hunt! And Woolmer, our inspired sculptor. And Millais, our host, *maître* and leader! Greetings, all! Ugh! Who would take a plain wife out in this foul weather, let alone an angel called Emily. Mother and child are crouching by a pathetic fire in Kentish Town and you haven't seen me lately because we are moving to Hampstead to get them out of this pestilential city. Only an angel could manage it with a

PROPOSAL FOR A HAPPY NEW YEAR.

Mr. Punch. "Good Bye! A Happy New Year to you?—(in Melipotamus)."

Mr Punch waves Cardinal Wiseman goodbye on a
Channel steam-packet back to his honorary bishopric
of 'Melipotamus' in the Middle East.

husband in my condition. But I had to drop in on my way home, for I bring the Brotherhood serious news and – aha, so this is a new masterpiece!'

He turned to the picture on the easel, a greenery-yellowy river scene of willows drooping over water gleaming in sunlight, an intricate composition of light and shade with, however, a large unpainted patch of prepared canvas in the centre.

'Something is missing and I think I can guess – do I see a lovely creature lying in the bath over there in a flowery robe? Is she dead? No, a model – *the* model I hear about? Introduce me, please!'

Warning Patmore not to touch the easel, Millais drew the poet to a large new zinc bath mounted on bricks at the end of the studio, in which lay the recumbent figure of a young woman with a soulful face whose dominant features were composed of passionate lips and huge grey eyes, framed by an unpinned mass of coppery hair.

'Miss Siddall, allow me to introduce Mr Coventry Patmore, of whom you have heard us speak with reverence. A man who knows England's acclaimed Poet Laureate, Tennyson himself, whose epic *In Memoriam* has opened, with Mr Patmore's poetry, a revolutionary era in English poetry just as we are doing in art. Mr Patmore, our loveliest model condescending to pose for me as Ophelia drowning in the river at Elsinore, Miss Elizabeth Siddall. Without whom the painting could not be painted. Please don't move, Miss Siddall. Is the cushion comfortable?'

'Guggums, whom I adore,' broke in Rossetti. 'Of course you can offer Mr Patmore your lily-white hand and shake that nimbus of flaming hair at him! You are not yet immersed, and brother Millais is merely working up his palette and his courage.' He put her slim fingers to his lips and presented her hand to Patmore to kiss likewise, which he had to kneel down to do. 'This is Guggums, dear Poet. Woolner here will make a medallion of her divine head as good as the one he's made of your own angel's flawless profile . . .'

'Aye, I will,' said Woolner. 'When Millais has drowned you.'

'How do you do, Miss Siddall?' said Patmore, hastily rising and sneezing again into a large red handkerchief.

'Pleased to meet you, sir,' said Miss Siddall faintly.

'Observe that hair,' declaimed Rossetti. 'It'll float in the water when Millais fills the bath – and so

> "Her clothes spread wide,
> And, mermaid-like, awhile they bore her up;
> Which time she chanted snatches of old tunes . . .
> Till that her garments, heavy with their drink,
> Pull'd the poor wretch from her melodious lay
> To muddy death."

'That's enough Shakespeare! I bet the bard had seen a corpse or two in the river, as I have. They don't usually float on their backs covered in flowers, but tend to lie face down and bloated . . .'

'And there are the flowers, in that bucket, for her garlands, so far as we could get any in this infernal weather, to stand in for Shakespeare's "crow-flowers, nettles, daisies and" . . . um . . . "long purples/That liberal shepherds give a grosser name,/But our cold maids do dead men's fingers call them". Shakespeare loved a bit of smut. Only the nettles are real nettles, the others are out of season . . .'

'But we've got an illustrated primer to copy from,' said Millais.

'You see, we follow nature with total fidelity according to the vows of our Brotherhood, my dear Patmore,' said Holman Hunt grimly.

'Her hair will float upon the glassy stream under the willows' hoar leaves, her bridal dress will be spread out suggestive of her winding-sheet,' declaimed Rossetti. 'The willows bowing like so many mourners – symbolism through absolute, almost casual, realism. To be precise, the purlieus of Surbiton. Potent. Compelling. Not like these bitumen brown, mud-coloured Academicians composing out of their sterile imaginations and never looking at anything real, how hair or drapery hangs, or how grass bends to the wind . . .'

'I hope the bath bit will fit in with the real brook,' said Woolner. 'Bit of a collage, really. One day we'll do it all by photography.'

'Oh, shut up! Of course we *ought* to put her in the water by the old bridge,' said Holman Hunt. 'But in this weather . . .'

'Miss Siddall will catch her death with perfect realism just in this bath,' said Patmore indignantly. 'Are you all mad? Yes, you are! I absolutely forbid it! Lying in a damp dress in icy water! I shall tell Emily . . . she'll never speak to you again.'

'Hold on, hold on, my dear, piteous man!' said Millais. 'Can't you see what's on the fire? We are heating up the water in kettles at this very minute, and you see this lamp – I shall light it under the bath and keep the water nice and warm. It would be better if we had hot water coming out of taps and could keep the temperature perfectly adjusted – I hear it is the latest luxury in rich people's houses, a hot-bath room! But we will keep Miss Siddall as warm as if she were taking Dr Gully's Malvern water treatment that Bulwer Lytton raves about. It's perfectly safe – he met a scientist called Darwin taking the treatment there . . .'

'Well, if Miss Siddall is prepared to take such risks for art's sake,' said Patmore doubtfully.

'Tell us your news,' said Woolner. 'If it's tin, we hold our hands out, we are skinned. A commission? Is that it? Do I see a commission in your face, oh heavenly poet who moveth among the mighty of this island of Pharisees? If not, I'm thinking of seeking my fortune in the Australian goldfields before I settle down to municipal statuary.'

'You do not,' said Patmore. 'And you are not likely to, I'm afraid. Your critics have found another stick to beat you with.'

'I thought they'd forgotten that it was my ugly father and mother who posed for Christ in the carpenter's shop, the swine – excuse me, Miss Siddall!' said Millais. 'I'll make *The Times* pay for that insult one day. A totally reverent conception of a real boy Christ helping his papa in a real carpenter's shop in Oxford Street!'

'And I'll kick their b—— . . . er, excuse me, Miss Siddall

– for what they said about my Christians sheltering a priest from the Druids,' said Hunt.

'That's just the trouble,' said Patmore. 'The story now is that the Pre-Raphaelite Movement is secretly part of the Tractarian treachery – worse, it is Romanist and popish propaganda, put out through you by the Jesuits. You know Charles Eastlake is likely to be president of the Academy next year? Well, he's sworn he'd never hang a subversive picture of the Pre-Raphaelite Brotherhood if he gets the job.'

'Well, damn them all to hell,' cried Rossetti. 'Excuse me, Guggums darling. It's my *Girlhood of Mary Virgin* that sets Protestant teeth on edge. No haloes. I bet that little beast Collinson is in it. Believe it or not, he's an art critic now.'

'He must live, and he certainly can't paint,' sighed Holman Hunt.

'Collinson? Wasn't he engaged to your sister, Gabriel?' asked Patmore.

'Yes, and when he went over to Rome in the summer, she broke it off. Christina is very High Church, you know, very. He's broken her heart. Her poetry is all about the happiness of dying forsaken. Very moving, beautiful. I'm against Christian piety myself. I am for Mazzini and heroic last-ditch defences, if anybody.'

'This Pope business has got nothing to do with art,' said Hunt. 'It's not High Church bishops versus popish superstition that's done this, it's the Academicians – Maclise and Landor and Egg and Frith, and that lot of dead-beats that we're showing up. They can't paint, their day is done and they know it. So they turn *The Times*, Eastlake and even Dickens against us. But what are we to do about it? Not to be hung is fatal.'

The others nodded gloomily.

Patmore said, 'I've one idea, if you're ready to risk it.' They were all interrogation. 'I might get Ruskin to look at your pictures – the ones that were hung last year and didn't sell, and your new ones like Ophelia in the river. If he didn't like them he'd say so and you'd all be finished for good.

But if he did like them he'd say so, and the critics would come round – fast. He's *the* critic, as you know. Nobody contradicts the author of *Modern Painters*! Nobody! Shall I try it? I do know him.'

'Get him. The PRB has nothing to fear,' said Hunt.

'Get him,' said Rossetti. 'I'll send him my *Early Italian Poets*.'

'I'll try it,' said Patmore. 'He's in Venice now. I'll try him when he comes back. That'll give you time to get your pictures ready. It's a risk, though. Ruskin knows everything worth knowing about painting and architecture.'

A timid voice came from the bath. 'I think the water is hot enough.'

'So it is,' shouted Millais. 'And the rest of you must clear out. I'm ready to start. Out! Out! Go and talk to my mother, but out!'

They rushed for their capes and mufflers.

8

The streets around the Guildhall were jam-packed with horses and carriages as the great and the good, the titled and the worthy, ministers of the Crown and ministers of the Church of England, merchant princes of the City and their ladies furbellowed, struggled to get through the doors and to find their places, while bands churned out patriotic airs. The New Police were everywhere, endlessly polite and tactful, milording and miladying the indignant or the confused.

The citizenry had cheered the Lord Mayor's Show, the troops, the floats, the African elephant, the gorgeously uniformed functionaries; now the quality's turn had come – to be feasted and to toast and be toasted, to hear speeches and spread gossip. This was the celebration of triumphant Trade, Shipping and Finance with which Britain held the world in fee. Ambassadors of the United States, Austria, France and Prussia take note!

Awaiting them was an army of waiters and two hundred and fifty tureens, each containing five pints of real turtle soup garnished with pies and suchlike side dishes, followed by eighty roast turkeys, six leverets, fifty pheasants, twenty-four geese, sixty dozens of partridges, fifteen dozens of wildfowl, heaps of vegetables and after that a hundred 30-pound pineapples, two hundred dozens of hothouse grapes, and a cornucopia of apples, peaches, pears, walnuts, savory cakes and ginger. Magnums of brandy and crates of fine clarets were opened to wash it all down with, not omitting the great loving-cup that went round and round . . . until at last the Lord Chancellor was hoisted to his feet and grimly stated that Protestant England had been invaded and occupied by a Roman hierarchy, accompanied by cheers of triumph, of domination, of insults and menaces. To this they would reply, he said, in the language of Shakespeare's Duke of Gloster:

'Under our feet we'll stamp thy Cardinal's Hat,
In spite of Pope or dignities of Church.'

He then sat down rather abruptly to thunderous cheers and Mr Delane, who, though not at the top table was of course well placed, gently banged on the table with his spoon, quietly prideful that such a warlike note had been masterminded by six weeks of leading articles in *The Times*.

Mr Disraeli thought this went a little far and was relieved when the Prime Minister, despite being received with another roll of thunderous cheers and banging of crested spoons, somewhat cooled the atmosphere by reassuring the chanceries of Europe that there would be no war against the invaders, as it was England's sacred task to preserve the peace of Europe; though a naval officer, proposing the toast of the Royal Navy, introduced the warning note that the country had the wherewithal to defend herself, at all times ready to strike, and retain the spoils of empire (some of which they had just tasted) flowing in and acreages of Lancashire cottons flowing out. Lord Palmerston, the conqueror of

Greece, pacifically toasted the ladies and their bright eyes – after all, he had been known as Lord Cupid in his far-off youth in those wild, mad Regency days.

Cardinal Wiseman was affronted by the coarse insults to his dignity at this vulgarian entertainment, but perceived that it provided a heaven-sent opportunity to hit back with all the resources of Christian casuistry. He booked space for his counter-attack in every news-sheet of note; *The Times*, too, had to print it, even though accompanied by the inevitable magisterial leading article rebutting it. His new bishops were protesting in their own pastorals that the uproar was instigated, besides being totally misconceived, as papists had no difficulty in giving to Caesar the things which were Caesar's – or Queen Victoria's – and to God the things which were God's; but the Cardinal went straight for the jugular.

So Britain prided herself on her constitutionality and in holding a man innocent until he was found guilty, did she? Yet the head and fount of the law had from the very Woolsack prejudged the issue, condemned the Roman Church as the aggressor without a fair trial, and had personally threatened to stamp on the headgear of an innocent shepherd who was as much a British subject and freeman as the Lord Chancellor himself. So who was the aggressor and law-breaker now, if you please?

Offensive things about rituals sacred to inoffensive Britons who happened to dissent in theological matters from the doctrines of the rich and privileged state Church had been voiced by the person who held the very helm of state and might therefore be expected to stand above abuse of a minority view, but instead had stirred the bigotry of the mob which had been ignited by a state clergy evidently in terror of a rival and the loss of its power, emoluments and privileges.

With the officers of public justice dead against us, the Cardinal went on, so that the doors of the Treasury itself might also be barred against us, the manly sense and honest heart of a generous (if heretical) people whose love of honest dealing, fair play and hatred of mean advantage taken, must now be our recourse. The new hierarchy abridged nobody's rights or freedom, but would confine its spiritual claims to its own followers and its temporal activities to succouring the poor and hungry in the foul slums which surrounded Westminster Cathedral (as they never did in pre-Reformation days, of course).

All we are doing, he added, is what the dissenters – the Scots Kirk, the Baptists, the Methodists, the Quakers, the Unitarians, the Independents, the Presbyterians – had done before them: disavow the state bishops and divide the country into convenient departments for ministering to their own followers. The creation of such 'sees' then had frightened nobody.

The Cardinal's counter-attack was considered by the thoughtful, the legal minds, and particularly by the literati of the realm, a skilful bit of pleading; and anyway there was nothing you could do to undo what had happened. Except to revoke the Catholic Emancipation Act of 1829, which would not be worthy of this enlightened nineteenth century, in which sweetness and light were being spread all over the world by British law, literature and civilisation, and by the example of liberal British capitalism and tutelage of lesser breeds without the law. Er, more or less. Well, were not paddle-steamers flying the white ensign chasing slavers in their clippers from the Bight of Benin to São Paulo and New Orleans?

But the *The Times* and lesser newspapers continued to be filled with the reports of indignation meetings up and down the country, headed not merely by the beneficed clergy, but by lords-lieutenant, magistrates, county magnates, aldermen, high sheriffs, provosts and even headmasters of schools when nobody else was handy to do so – the nation's respected leaders of opinion, all repeating *The Times*'s successive retorts to the Cardinal's arguments, leading article by leading article (often three a week). Moreover, the dissenters did not appreciate the Cardinal's equating of their forms of dissent with his, but protested and memorialised the Queen almost as much as the beneficed churchmen. Everything said was reported in full by the column, even the foolhardy protests by the odd papist in the audience, and however repetitive proved good copy; besides which many organisations took advertising space to hammer home their points, to the considerable advantage of the paper's profit-and-loss account.

Still, so far, only one of the Cardinal's coach's windows had been broken by a flying half-brick flung by a militant dissenter.

It was upsetting, none the less, for the Cardinal to find that members of his own flock exercised the rights of Englishmen to stab him in the back in letters to *The Times*, impudently signing themselves as 'A Catholic'. Could they be fraudulent, he wondered? But no, they would at once insist that they had an Englishman's right to have a hierarchy, however unwanted, and at the same time to reveal that he received his Catholic callers on their knees while he lounged in a luxurious armchair, and made them stand, even old ladies, until His Eminence left the room. Another otherwise loyal defender of the Faith wrote that the only thing that was objectionable about the new hierarchy was Wiseman himself, a disastrous choice who was known to be vain, ambitious and pompous, loving power and speaking the language of pride and dominion over everybody else, assuming that the English nation was at his feet – a people of whom he knew nothing. Another appalling letter exposed the questions that were officially required to be asked by confessors about their female penitents' sexual thoughts and behaviour, stopping little short of the pornography peddled in Holywell Street.

And then in Birkenhead a protest meeting was completely wrecked by the sticks and stones of hundreds of Irish dockers and shipbuilders, ordered to be at the meeting by their local priest, one Father Brown. Two policemen were reported killed, and dozens of "Prots" given black eyes and other nasty contusions. So, thundered *The Times*, and most of the rest of the press and almost every Protestant pulpit, this is what is meant by a purely spiritual supremacy, once the Catholic Church is in a majority anywhere in England. Father Brown denied liability: it was all the fault of Protestant aggression, said he, in an area where Catholic susceptibilities ought to have been respected. . . .

To top it all the Duke of Norfolk, England's premier Catholic peer, Master of the Horse and Chamberlain of the Court, wrote to say that ultramontanism (as professed by the Cardinal) was incompatible with the oath of allegiance to the Queen. It was vexing, to say the least, especially as a Mr Cummins was able to reveal that the oath of allegiance to the Queen (as required by the Emancipation Act of 1829) had been deleted from the form of words voiced by the Cardinal at his historic induction at Westminster.

However, Archdeacon Manning was surely if slowly coming in, even if some of the other converts were not of the first quality. What they really needed was to win over Gladstone, who unfortunately happened to be investigating prison conditions in Naples and so not immediately approachable. But there was John Henry Newman. He was asked to prepare lectures and sermons which, in his inimitable manner, would destroy the Church of England's moral position from Queen Elizabeth's time to the present day, with emphasis on hanging, drawing and quartering of innocent Catholics. Among his friends Newman intimated that he felt that the installation of the hierarchy was inopportune, but prepared to obey instructions.

Christmas was now approaching, and *The Times* was able to claim that the volume of spontaneous protest had not slackened even after two months had passed. The nation had spoken with 'unparalleled unanimity'. It was high time for the Government's response. The statute under which the Pope could defy the feelings of the English people with impunity must be revised, if his plans to control England as he already controlled Ireland were to be nipped in the bud. The Pope had said 'I will' and the people of England had said, with *The Times*, 'You will not.'

So what are they going to do, asked Mr Delane as he smiled his inscrutable smile at Broadlands, at Bath House, at

Devonshire House, in Carlton House Terrace, as ministers forgathered and indicated, without details, that the matter was well in hand. Wiseman would be on his way back to Rome in the new year.

9

'Well, you've talked with the law lords. What do they say you can do, dear?' said Lady Russell, as they stood in Hyde Park observing Mr Paxton's men erecting the Crystal Palace.

She had been to see it before, but Lord John had been too busy; besides, he was afraid he might meet somebody on the site who would ask him exactly that question. That ghastly man Greville, for instance. But the weather was awful and there was a chance he could get away with it. He really had to see it, because somebody was sure to ask him at a dinner party during the Christmas holiday if he thought it would blow down in the first gale of wind. He had to be ready to say 'I have seen it, and I have been assured it will be perfectly safe.' In the tone of voice he would say this there would be no possibility of asking him further idiotic questions about it. He half hoped it *would* fall down, as the excitement would divert attention from Wiseman, particularly if there were a heavy loss of life. They had snatched the opportunity while the carriages were being loaded in Richmond for the trip to Woburn. There he would be comparatively inaccessible.

He was, in fact, aching to leave. He felt ill, exhausted. He needed a longish rest to be ready to meet the House in the new year. A hundred times a day, it felt as if people had said to him, 'What are you going to do about Wiseman?' – increasingly and ominously, 'the Cardinal?' – and a hundred times he had replied, in his iciest tone, 'Wait and see.' What was worse, he had said it to Lady Russell a good many times as well. He wished she would stay even longer in Pembroke

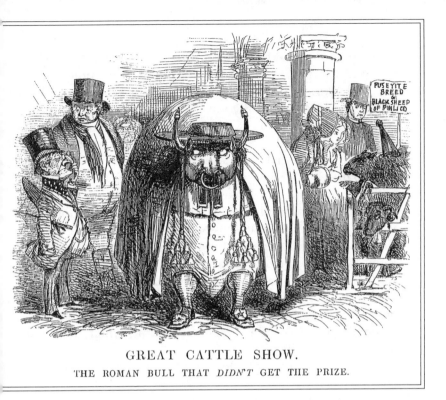

PUSEYITE
BREED
OR
BLACK SHEEP
OF PIMLICO

GREAT CATTLE SHOW.
THE ROMAN BULL THAT *DIDN'T* GET THE PRIZE.

Punch puns the papal 'bull' entered for the prize in
the English cattle show (with the small Puseyite black
sheep also being entered).

Lodge with the children. What with his first wife's four, and Fanny still industriously producing, there were now nine of them. He hated to see Fanny in No. 10; when she wasn't talking about Wiseman she was asking him what he was going to do about the crumbling ruin in Downing Street. Was he expected to spend his own money on that impossible house? His brother Bedford could reasonably be asked to pay for the repairs; but he was mean beyond belief. Parsimony ran in the family, but the Duke was the worst yet.

He peered round to see if anyone was near enough to overhear. Blessedly nobody was. 'The law lords are agreed that Wiseman has done nothing illegal unless we accuse him under Thirteen Queen Elizabeth, Clause two, which Baring wants us to do. If convicted, that would involve our cutting off his head, possibly hanging, drawing and quartering him. How stupid can you be? Even if the court convicted, he would then ask for the Queen's pardon, which he would get. And then what?'

'The Queen cannot pardon him unless you and the Home Secretary . . .'

'Try not to be ridiculous, Fanny dear. I've got a hell of a headache this morning.'

'My poor darling. You are worn out. What does the Queen think, then?'

'You mean what does Prince Albert think? I have persuaded the Prince not to imagine that though laws passed three hundred years ago may well be valid in Prussia and Austria, they are not necessarily still applicable here.'

'Yet the Prince always seems to be so full of ideas. Like this glasshouse, for instance. Though don't you think, if they really are going to build it high enough to enclose those elm trees, it will be blown down in a high wind? That's why I asked you to have a look at it, dear.'

'The Prince's idea is that I should reconstruct the Cabinet and bring the Peelites in. Especially Gladstone.'

'Has he not suggested that before?'

'He has. More than once. He thinks that unless I bring in

Gladstone, the first storm of the next session will blow the Government down.'

'Surely not?'

'Not if the Cabinet supports me.'

'It will, won't it? Over Wiseman?'

'Oh yes. If we do nothing, Grey, and his four loathsome relatives, and Carlisle and Labouchere will stick.'

'Then what, dear? Are you going to admit defeat, after all these protest meetings?'

'Certainly not. We are going to change the law.'

'Aha! And the Cabinet is agreed?'

'Certainly not. It never is. A crisis impends.'

'I feared so. It's a frightful Cabinet.'

'It is. But it's the only one I've got.'

'Who will resign?' she asked him tremulously.

'Nobody will. Grey, Carlisle and Labouchere foresee defeat. But they will stay. Pam, of course. Baring – well, I told you about him. The sailor boy! So will Wood, busy fiddling with the budget. Lansdowne is disgusted with Lord Chancellor Truro, but will stick. Basically nobody wants to do anything. But I told them that a government ought not to be the only body of politicians who could propose nothing, so we had to bring in a bill to trip up Wiseman . . . the Attorney-General – what's his name? – has got a good idea.'

'Yes?' breathed his wife.

'We will make any ecclestiastic who takes a territorial title without the agreement of the Government and the Queen liable to a fine of one hundred pounds, and that any financial arrangement made with such a person shall be null and void. Roughly that's it. The Attorney-General thinks it will do the job.'

'But . . . is that all?'

Her husband nodded vigorously as he watched iron window-frames hoisted high into the air.

'It means that the twelve bishoprics they've announced will have to be paid for, how often has to be decided, but anyway it will be horribly humiliating for them. The real penalty is that so long as they call themselves Bishop of this and that, no money and no property can pass into their hands – notably into Archbishop Wiseman's, which really will hurt because he expects to have at his sole disposal all the property the Catholic institutions have got, and hope to get in future from the bequests of their communicants, some of whom are very rich! The priest who gives absolution to a dying millionaire has a lot of influence over deathbed codicils! It's money that confers power. I am told that in Italy the Church's property and land is the basis of the Pope's power. King Victor Emmanuel of Savoy wants to tax them, and they refuse to pay. Why, it was the Church's vast possessions that prompted Henry VIII to side with the Reformation – that and marrying Anne Boleyn, of course. But we needn't dwell on all that. We just give them a reminder that the Reformation hasn't lost its sting. It will leave the Romanists in about the position of the Baptists, which isn't much. A clever scheme, I rather think. They will back off. Then at last perhaps we can get on with parliamentary reform next session. That I have sworn I shall do!'

Her Ladyship clapped her hands. 'It sounds marvellous, John! The slap of firm government at last!'

'Let's get back to the lodge, dear. And remember, it is not all over bar the shouting. The country will be behind us, but the House is not the country, and Dizzy is watching for the moment to bring us down. The Prince sees that. It's why he wants me to strengthen the Cabinet. Unfortunately, the only men who have the backing in the House that I need are all opposed to penalties against religious freedom to do what you like. And throw my reputation as a liberal in my face. Even the Radicals are split – Ashley says I have a duty to God to save Protestantism from Wiseman. Roebuck says I am antagonising Ireland for ever. The only thing they agree on is higher wages for the workers. Where's our brougham? Let's get back. I feel awful. Haven't slept for two nights.'

In the brougham they snuggled together under the rugs.

68

Lady Russell cuddled the little man, murmuring, 'You will win, my darling. Your plan is masterly, and what is more, it is morally right: God will back you up. But you must conserve your poor strength. Now, don't be with cross with me. I have an idea. There's a doctor who can give you the relaxation and the sleep that you need to recruit your mental forces. Not like *our* doctor....'

The Prime Minister stirred uneasily.

'You don't mean Dr Gully's water treatment, dear? I couldn't stand it. He would kill me, no matter what Bulwer Lytton was telling me.'

'No, no. But you mustn't be angry, I've been talking to Harriet. I know you don't like her but she does hear everything. She knows the Carlyles...'

'Who doesn't?' the Prime Minister said peevishly. 'Those *Latter-Day Pamphlets* were aimed at me. Good as called me an incompetent nincompoop.'

'You know they both suffer from insomnia, constipation and indigestion.'

'Well? Many do nowadays.'

'He was having breakfast with Monckton Milnes a week or so ago, and had a frightful stomach pain. Appalling, apparently. Well, there happened to be a Dr Ashburner there, who is a qualified man but also a practising mesmerist. Carlyle and his wife are bitterly against that sort of thing, they tried it before with him. Actually, they hate the idea of being put to sleep by anyone else. Loss of personal responsibility they call it, betrayal of the human will. Carlyle was telling Harriet about it. But it worked. Immediately, total relief! Of course his wife gave him laudanum too, they both take it in buckets, Harriet says, but that didn't work until later. Just think. My dear, forgive me, I have had a talk with Dr Ashburner, a most gentlemanly person. About the will, and how you can lend it to a properly trained therapist, to use it for you to cure yourself. Carlyle calls it devil's magic, but Dr Ashburner says it is the latest discovery of medical science ... and people always denounce the latest discoveries, especially the medical profession. He says for some cases it is better and far safer than chloroform. I think we should look into it, ask him to come to Richmond – I will let him try it out on me first. He is a very religious man, otherwise I wouldn't. Now, just to please me . . .'

'Well, we'll see. Ain't this mesmerism stuff one of the famous Miss Martineau's fads?'

10

Mr Thackeray, shrouded with smoke from the funnel above him, stood watching the three-master *Derwent* making for midstream, her decks crowded with waving emigrants, Australia-bound. Near him in the stern sheets of the river steamer, Westminster-bound, sat an artist, Mr Madox Brown, a Pre-Raphaelite, sketching from the life this affecting scene, seeking to fix exactly the expressions on white, tearful faces straining to catch the last glimpse of England as she faded into the fog. It was a scene he could sketch almost every day as ship after ship leaves the homeland, lightening it of its overload of unemployed and poverty-stricken proletarians, in obedience to the bidding of economists and Malthusians as well as the lure of new-found gold on those farther shores.

Mr Thackeray himself had a few words with the artist, mentioning that he himself did a little sketching for *Punch*, whither he himself was bound, to put into words, with wit and human touches, he hoped, these signs of a burgeoning empire being peopled by the island race; he mentioned to Mr Brown that a baby was born in one of the cabins minutes before *Derwent* cast off. Mr Brown said, 'Make a nice touch if one could get it into a picture, done inboard. Damn this smoke.'

Already, as the paddles churned the stinking water, phrases for a five-pound column of reflections on emigration formed themselves in Mr Thackeray's mind. 'They are quitting that Gothic society, with its ranks and hierarchies, its cumbrous

70

ceremonies, its glittering antique paraphernalia in which we have been educated ... leaving this country and escaping from the question of the prospering rich versus the desperate poor, but what of the fate of us who remain to face the music?' Lemon would find it a trace heavy, perhaps, but he was getting tired of the fulminations against the Cardinal and the Romanists that he had spat out for so many weeks; he could surely leave that for a bit to the Protestant fanatics led by Lord Ashley. After all, if Wiseman was allowed to set up a granite statue of the BV in the Strand which Dr Newman was required to insist actually wept on holy days, while scrutinising scientists proved it did no such impossible thing, might that not do more to bring the whole nonsense down in a gale of wholesome laughter than anything *Punch* could publish? By their miracles shall ye know them.

After he'd earned his fiver or so, he had to finish *Pendennis*. Praise be, the last two numbers would be – must be! – out before Christmas. It was selling well, ending sentimentally on its predestined 'happy ever after' note.

But was it true to life? He'd asked himself that from time to time. Was it a fair picture of a young man's moral battle with himself through scrapes and follies that never involved him in actual vice? Pendennis was W.M.T. himself in much of the tale; but *he* had not passed through temptation unsmirched, had he? Did *any* young man about town, making his way in life, as he passed the temptations in the streets or behind the scenes at the opera? Then why pretend he did so, adventuring but unspotted? But no, that must not be written of, *virginibus puerisque*!

Would writers ever again be allowed even the minor licence of his beloved eighteenth century – much less the pagan truths hidden behind the inanities of the forbidden books? Would the truth ever be told by some future generation of novelists about men, women, sex and marriage? And if not, if one could write only under the censorship of this Mrs Grundy who walked, impervious of bowdlerising, the gaslit highways of our Sodom and Gomorrah, what was the point of writing?

71

Of literature? Just to amuse idle women with fairy-tales?

What of the purity of his own brother-and-sister relationship with another man's wife which torments and frustrates him? As the extra man whose jealous passion was masked behind a bantering wit: the tinkle of his cap and bells proclaiming his safeness – his emasculation! Pendennis! Why not write the whole humiliating story – and choose a franker century to set the action in . . . could this be the germ of his next novel: another beautiful and desirable Jane, another uncaring, insensitive, pietistic William, another faithful and attendant – but virile – Thackeray. . . ?

It was going to be a drab Christmas. First he must put in an appearance at the funeral of young Henry Hallam, whose coffin had now reached Clevedon from Italy, dead of malaria – and *she* would be there too, lovely and unattainable, but irresistible as an itch demanding to be scratched. That torment over, he had planned to spend Christmas in Paris and to take his daughters to his mother to care for there while he renewed his acquaintance among the great – Louis Napoleon and Thiers; the stimulating and amusing, like George Sand, Dorsay and Dumas, and those charmers who would be called the *demi-monde* or worse in London: actresses and cocottes and the rest of the passing Parisian show to divert his starved soul and provide copy for articles. But, alas, he couldn't go.

He had been forced to cancel the trip because once again he was without a governess for his two motherless daughters, Anny and Minny. Ever since that infernal novel *Jane Eyre* by the Brontë authoress had been published, describing how her hero, the romantic Mr Rochester, had a mad wife hidden away and planned bigamously to marry the governess of his ward, the gossips had speculated at Mr Thackeray's relations with the governesses he employed to look after his daughters – his wife, too, being mad. The gossips – that is, everybody – saw each governess as a potential mistress or even bigamously married wife of W.M.T., so one after another he had dismissed the poor wretches when the gossip got too hot . . . and after Christmas he was to engage yet another.

And all this just when the sudden demise of his Aunt Frances had compelled him to offer a temporary home, at least for the Christmas holidays, to her two motherless sons . . . so, with no governess in residence to preserve the proprieties, the proprieties required him to spend Christmas in Kensington and organise some appropriate recreations for them all.

And he could feel another of his winter bad colds coming on. . . .

11

It was another foggy morning. The street lamps glowed dimly, the cabs drove cautiously. Mr Pugin's Gothic windows in St George's, Southwark, filtered the daylight feebly; within, the church was sombre and Gothic, as Mr Pugin would have wished, despite the modern lamps in the lustres. Movement, murmuring, could be heard; processions were being marshalled and instructed. Then, outside, there was a muffled clatter of hoofs and wheels; lights flickered in the streets all the way from Golden Square as torch-bearers escorted the gilded coach of the Cardinal Archbishop, drawn by six fine bays, to a jingling halt outside the cathedral where the enthronement was to take place. (St George's became a cathedral the very moment Westminster had an archbishop, naturally.) The route had not been exactly lined by rejoicing crowds, and a group of loiterers by the entrance raised only a subdued cheer. As yet no proper acclamations for suchlike solemnities of Holy Church. Not yet!

But within, the event was taking shape. An acolyte approached down the nave with a thurifer; a great crucifix was carried to the spot where the procession of the clergy of the archdiocese was finally to form; a bell tolled to tell them to form and they shuffled and frou-froued into formation; a chalice was carried from one altar to another. Then His Eminence the Cardinal himself, having emerged

73

from the coach and entered the sacristry, where he was robed in scarlet and white and capped with a small scarlet cap, advanced from the sacristry into the nave, his long train borne up by two train-bearers; whereupon the choir burst into the Hallelujah from Beethoven's 'Mount of Olives'. The procession moved slowly forward. An impressive canopy, fringed with silk and gold, was borne over his path followed by two hundred recent converts from the Church of England, proud of the witness they were giving to the true Faith, absolved of their sins, their heresy abjured. After them came the members of the various religious orders, among whom the Oratorians were conspicuous in their striking habits, and among them might be discerned the presence of the famous Dr Newman. Lastly came Dr Doyle in sacrificial vestments. At the rood-screen the Cardinal entered the chapel of the Blessed Eucharist, participated in the rites, moved to the altar, knelt and participated in the prayers; whereafter the mitre was placed on his head and the crozier placed in his hand. He was assisted to the archepiscopal chair, at the foot of which the whole body of clergy prostrated themselves and made obeisance to him as the papal bull installing him was read: Nicholas, by the title of St Pudentiana, Cardinal, Priest, Archbishop of Westminster in the United Kingdom of Great Britain and Ireland.

Many unbelievers, reading the account in considerable (if sometimes inaccurate) detail in *The Times* and lesser papers the following morning, found their breakfasts spoiled; nor were they much mollified by learning that St Pudentiana was the daughter of a Roman senator, Servilius Pudens, whose wife was Claudia, daughter of the conquered British king Caractacus and at whose hospitable Christian table St Paul had been a frequent guest. Sainthood had naturally rubbed off on her and there was in Rome a church dedicated to her, sealing the tie between Rome and Britain which thereby became a hereditament of the Pope.

Many an egg went cold, and many a dish of kidneys or kedgeree also lost their savour the following week when *The*

Times reported the Cardinal's jeers from his pulpit at the Protestant remonstrances against the insults to the Queen's sovereignty: 'Suppose anyone had told you six months ago that the Bishop of Rome had it in his power to shake a vast empire into convulsions from throne to hearth, from cathedral to cottage; to upheave by the breath of his nostrils the granite foundations of the noble British constitution, to shake at its base the throne of our gracious Queen, to despoil of its rights and prerogative a church which has a thousand roots in the very substance of the nation, to introduce into everything that has been a popular bugbear in popery into your very families. If someone had told you that a pope could do all this by changing the name of a bishop of Tracia to Bishop of Beverley, and a bishop of Tioa to Bishop of Liverpool, would you not have laughed to scorn a man who told you he had such tremendous power? . . .'

'He would if he could! That's the just way he'd like it!' snarled the infuriated at their breakfast-tables.

And in full canonicals he had the gall, it was reported, to carry papal good wishes and Christmas cheer on foot to the dwellers in those rookeries which festered between the precincts of Westminster Abbey and the precincts of the South-Eastern Counties railway terminus abutting Buckingham Palace Road; and a well-known layman accompanied his retinue. 'Here,' the Cardinal said, making a magisterial sweep with his crozier. 'Somewhere here, anyway, we shall buy up these foul slums and flatten them to make a noble piazza for our metropolitan cathedral, probably dedicated to St Pudentiana. Something bigger than the Abbey, don't you think, Mr Pugin?'

'The greatest cathedral in England, of course.' said Mr Pugin. 'I mean, the greatest Gothic cathedral, of course. One ignores St Paul's.'

'Gothic?' queried the Cardinal. 'I was thinking of something more Italian – romanesque. Assisi, Perugia? We must get our people to be Italian in mood and surroundings.'

'Gothic, Your Eminence, Gothic. If you want to think Italian, think of Milan. But I think of fourteenth-century English. Otherwise you might as well put up something like that glasshouse in Hyde Park. Never! I shall draw the designs for you.'

'I suppose it would take some time to build – money has to be collected.'

'Of course it will take some time to build! Probably two hundred years or more. Whoever heard of a complete cathedral being built in the life of one man? These great structures have been the work of centuries, begun by one founder and carried to completion by his successors through change and modified architectural style and technique – but not like that blot, that glass monstrosity that disfigures Hyde Park, bolted together by a jobbing gardener and a Birmingham ironmaster – God save us all!'

'Quite so, Mr Pugin, quite so,' said His Eminence. He had not felt so abashed since he had arrived in England.

However, back in Golden Square, he later had the satisfaction of exercising, in a preliminary but significant matter, his temporal power. He had been told that there was a case for his intervention in a chancery suit to the advantage of the Church's funds. A French resident, one M. Mathurian Carée, had settled in Somerstown and by hard work and frugality had by the time of his death amassed £10,000, which by will he had bequeathed to the Church for a female educational charity. This he had done in a deed of gift made out for him with a power of attorney by a priest who had providentially though unasked attended his deathbed, and who, making off with both the deed and the power of attorney, had hastily had the funds transferred to the Church's keeping: so hastily, in fact, that the holy father had not had time to stay to shrive him.

Highly irregular, very regrettable; but one could hope that in consideration of his dying action in bequeathing his all to holy charity M. Carée had been put in a state of penitence sufficient to fit his soul to be received into eternal life. Unhappily his relatives in France learned of his bequest, and, calling witnesses (including his landlady and Dr Gasquet his medical adviser) to show that he had sedulously refrained from going to church or attending mass, had frequently been heard to revile priests and the priesthood, and had shown scarcely less animus against womenkind, had brought suit in Chancery to impeach the bill as made under undue pressure and have the £10,000 paid into court without prejudice.

The Cardinal had felt he must take it on himself to oppose, with the Church's legal advisers, the Chancery suit, as an outrageous attempt by M. Carée's relatives to grab the money freely given to the Church and thus even risk his very salvation. By making suitable arrangements with his ecclesiastical opposite numbers in France, the Cardinal Archbishop was able to bring the relatives (whom M. Carée evidently also much disliked) to a better frame of mind, and the money was amicably if unevenly divided between them and the Church, so that the suit was withdrawn and the scandal of a Chancery case avoided. The Cardinal was able to take satisfaction in the thought that but for his elevation to equal rank with the Archbishop of Paris, the necessary pressure on the relatives' defective consciences might not have been made available.

What wasn't avoided was the unwelcome publicity given to the story by the press, which cast aspersions that might also have been actionable had not that course risked predictable imputations of an open demonstration of the new hierarchy's temporal power and spiritual arm-twisting.

And there was bad news in the wind in the new year. The Cardinal's intelligence network at length came through with the Cabinet's decision on what it was going to do about the so-called 'papal aggression' when Parliament met. He learned that it intended to propose that anyone taking a territorial title not authorised by the Crown would have to pay a fine for so doing: probably £100. Humiliating, said the Cardinal, but it could be treated as a form of persecution and a violation of the Emancipation Act of 1829 – even as martyrdom, if one were put in jail for refusing to pay. What was really intolerable, however, was the proposal to make such taking of territorial titles a legal bar to receiving or controlling money entrusted to, or settled on the Church. It would mean that moneys, like those from M. Carée's bequest, could not be passed on to the Cardinal Archbishop to administer as he saw fit – and much, oh, so much more! *This* was a deadly, fiendish blow; an axe laid to the root of the hierarchy's function – to its spiritual supremacy, in fact. At a stroke, for instance, the orders, like the Benedictine monasteries and schools and the Jesuits, would be able to do what they liked with their money without any reference, let alone discussion, with the new hierarchy.

If, that is, the Government got such a piece of brutal, intolerant and prescriptive legislation through the House.

'It must not go through,' thundered Cardinal Archbishop Wiseman, storming up and down his study. 'It shall not go through. *No pasarán!* Monsignor Searle, make me a list of every Catholic peer in the House of Lords – and every Catholic MP. Every Catholic in the administration of this bigoted country, every Catholic officer, at least from majors upwards, in the armed forces, any rich Catholic business men, I know we have some! Well, you know what I want. Go to it.'

His private secretary bowed deeply and made for the door.

'Stop! One minute!' shouted His Eminence. 'Put on the list every fanatical, evil-thinking liberal person with influence. You know what I mean – the Radicals! Roebuck! Cobden! Bright! Graham! Oh, Gladstone! If necessary, meet Gladstone's boat at Dover!'

Slowly, His Eminence eased himself into his chair. 'So Johnny Russell thinks he can get his own way in government, in his own Cabinet, does he? We'll see. Oh, we'll see!'

To make assurance doubly sure he knelt down and raised his hands in supplication.

LORD JACK THE GIANT KILLER.

Mr Punch and John Bull cheer on Lord John Russell,
armed with the shining sword of the Ecclesiastical
Titles Assumption Bill against Wiseman, armed with
his crook, in single combat.

12

They were all back in town now. From the hunting field, from the racing, from the coursing, from Paris, from the Scottish moors, from Switzerland, from Windsor, for the opening of Parliament. Lady Palmerston's reception-rooms in Carlton House Terrace were packed with them. Haw-hawing, chortling, murmuring, nodding, giggling – giggle, giggle, trill, trill. Male talk, female talk, baritone and falsetto, behind grins, behind beards, behind fans, gossip and chatter: all of it false, false! Why was one here? To be seen, to be heard, but above all to be seen in a new and memorable evening *grande tenue* and jewels: that was all. But *why* was she here, what was she *for. . . ?*

'Miss Florence Nightingale, I believe?'

A slight curtsy – she had not the faintest idea who he was, an MP probably, possibly a peer; not a prelate or officer in uniform; bald pate, clean-shaven, heavy eyebrows, chin like a warship's ram – must be a professor; but who, or of what, she had no idea.

'This place is as noisy as a cotton mill!' He shouted. 'We have met, Miss Nightingale. In Oxford, a few years ago. You and your father came to call on Lord and Lady Lovelace, and I happened to be there. I am Charles Babbage . . .'

'Professor Babbage!' She apologised gracefully for her hesitation. What a summer that had been! And *he* was there, walking with her in the college garden. . . . 'I remember I upset you! I told you that I'd been trying to learn algebra, and you said "Well, why not?" and I said "Because my mother considers algebra unladylike." And, Professor, you were very wroth!' She was smiling the party smile again.

'I was furious, absolutely furious. As though it was unladylike to do anything whatsoever with a lady's brain but construct embroidery. Look, Miss Nightingale, over there – there *is* Ada Lovelace herself. What's remarkable about her, eh?'

Miss Nightingale looked. She thought of saying 'She looks remarkably ill!' but paused. Ada Lovelace looked terrible, hardly recognisable as the woman who had so charmed her five years ago at Oxford. She could say, as anybody else would, 'She's Lord Byron's daughter', but she refrained.

'I ought to know, but . . .'

'She happens to be the finest mathematician in Britain – probably in Europe. 'That's what *her* brains are for. Not for calculating betting odds – that was her mistake. No, not for that, poor dear. But for helping me build my computing machine, the greatest invention of this century of invention!'

Florence was about to say 'I will speak with her' and move away through the crush, but the Professor hung on to her.

'And why am *I* here, wasting my time in this bedlam? To have a word with the next prime minister, Lord Palmerston.'

'Lord Palmerston prime minister? I have heard Lord John was having problems, but . . .'

'Johnny Russell is finished! He'll be out in a few weeks. Pam will come in. He's the man the people want. And when he comes in I want to get him to renew the government subsidy necessary to complete my computing engine, with Ada's help if she's still up to it. Oh yes, she's had problems, but you know she's Byron's daughter, don't you? Streak of madness in that family, eh? But madness is cousin to genius. She's got to help me finish the machine, and Pam's got to give us the money we need.'

Florence still wanted to move in Ada Lovelace's direction, though she was hidden for the moment by Lord Carlisle and Sir James Graham trying to make themselves heard. She said, 'This invention, it's not finished?'

'Nearly. And when it is . . .'

'You'll show it at the Great Exhibition, I suppose?'

'Pah! That senseless affair. No, I'll conquer the world with it.'

'Really? What will your invention do, Professor?'

'Add, subtract, multiply, divide, solve equations . . .'

'Something for mathematicians, then. . . ?' She made to move; Ada was slipping out of reach.

'For statisticians, Miss Nightingale, statisticians. This is the age of statistics, and we need machines to sort them, rapidly and accurately and humanely – saving those poor wretches who are losing their eyesight adding up columns of figures, often wrongly. The things we need to know, and don't, because we haven't enough clerks, locked up in great heaps of unanalysed statistics. . . .'

His eyes had the mad gleam of the fanatic. She was held, and said, 'But what use . . .'

'Use! In everything. In the budget that fool Wood is getting ready.' (Sir Charles Wood was confabulating with Carlisle and Graham now. Ada had disappeared.) 'In knowing what you've got, where and how much – in war, for example. That I will explain to Pam. You look puzzled. Well, just imagine this: you have an army in the field. Dozens of regiments, horses, guns; no good at all without a proper supply of ammunition, food, equipment, tents, medical supplies for the wounded, transport – an immense vocabulary of requirements and one that varies, and must be changed, with changes in the enemy's own dispositions. And that is why my machine will do it for you. You give the machine the whole huge requirement, it calculates almost instantly what must be provided and sent – and, for example, if the losses prove to be heavy, how much more of a thousand requirements must be supplemented, and how fast! Which means you're always better equipped to fight than your enemy is . . .'

'But there is no war, Professor, fortunately.'

'There will be. That was just an example. Meanwhile there are hundreds of uses for my machine in commerce.'

He was holding her arm now, pouring out his words. 'I don't know how long it took Paxton to calculate what quantities of iron and glass he needed for his glasshouse, but whatever it needed, all that he reckoned up in a day, my calculating difference engine would work out in an hour.'

Miss Nightingale was impressed, the noise and the crush forgotten. 'But how,' she began, only to find the Professor turning his back on her. 'There's Pam,' he cried, 'Excuse me, I must catch him.' He clove through the crowd without ceremony.

Lady Lovelace was now nowhere to be seen. But she could help to design a great machine! She was a woman who *did* things, who didn't mind working her fingers to the bone, evidently.

The old discontent swept over her again. People greeted her, she responded like a great calculating engine; it clicked (clicked?) out her stereotyped replies for her as she stood back and day-dreamed . . . and then the dream took on form and the machine vanished: *he* was approaching her through the crush. Yes, Mr Monckton Milnes, MP, a faint smile on his lips.

How fast can memories create themselves: scenes, conversations, feelings, decisions, all made over years gone by, while one human being takes six or seven steps towards you, and colour in seconds suffuses your cheeks. The man who wanted to marry her, asked her again and again and had been refused every time. And, refused, had inhabited her day-dreams inexorably and persistently as the passionate Other; with whom in dreams she had had so many adventures, with whom in dreams she had shamelessly done things that she hardly knew how she knew how to do: everything that God had forbidden her while she reserved herself to do some great task to honour Him. Yet always she had imagined that if that Voice had been deceiving her, that if she could no longer wait for that promised fulfilment, she could turn to this man and flesh out the dream as wife, mother, inspiration. On his arm, at his side, helping with some great design, some great parliamentary reform bill perhaps. . . .

He drew level, bowed slightly, but did not stop.

'Miss Nightingale. What a noise, like a cotton mill, eh?' And walked on. Walked on, as if they were but slight acquaintances. Walked on, leaving her to turn hastily to someone else to be seen talking to, not to be seen even for a moment apparently neglected.

He had finished with her. She forced back her tears and made for her mother and Parthe who would hate to be so long parted from her even in Lady Palmerston's levee. The man she adored, the man she expected always to respond to her, to adore her notwithstanding his rejection, his Beatrice, his Egeria, his adored but untouchable friend – finished with her!

Another pair of eyes were fixed on her as she struggled to get away. A tall, elderly, authoritative figure. His voice was low and strangely commanding.

'Forgive me speaking. Let it go. Do not fear. You have, I detect, a tremendous magnetic power, but in the negative phase. That will be reversed, and destines you to great things, for it cannot be negated much longer.'

She stared at the stranger who accosted her, trying but unable to compose the haughty expression his intrusion demanded. He was proffering his card as she turned away.

'I am Dr Ashburner. If – when I can help you, my consulting-room is in Grosvenor Street. . . .'

13

'Well, Prime Minister, what am I going to say?'

'With Your Majesty's gracious agreement, your government proposes that the speech from the throne shall first point to the maintenance of peace with your foreign neighbours, emphasising our – that is, Your Majesty's – satisfaction with the treaty that has ended the conflict in Denmark averting the risk of a European war, and with . . . er . . . our treaty with . . . um . . . Sardinia, leading up to Your Majesty's assurances to your subjects' innumerable petitions that you will maintain your sovereignty against the aggression of the P——— . . . I mean, of a certain foreign prince, and Parliament will be asked to give the Government leave to bring in a bill, the details of which will be revealed in due course, followed by mention of the unparalleled economic prosperity your country enjoys, perhaps apart from the, ahem, landowners, a law for the registration of deeds and, and, er . . . that's it, Your Majesty.'

There was a silence, leaving Lord John Russell feeling even more than usual like a naughty boy. It was deathly cold in the palace withdrawing-room, and he wished he had put on an extra vest and a second pair of drawers under his court dress, but that was probably too tight anyway. It seemed to have unaccountably shrunk in the last wash. At last came the inevitable question, 'What do you think, Albert dear?'

'Apart from the Pope bit, rather thin, *Liebchen.*'

There was another silence. Then Her Majesty said, 'Thinnish, Prime Minister?'

'I am sure Your Majesty knows my ambition is to bring in a substantial measure extending the parliamentary franchise to, ah, responsible persons only, of course. But we feel, at least *I* feel, that such a reform requires more preparation, and should await the next session. Our time this session will be more than filled by the Ecclesiastical Titles Assumption Bill.'

'Yes,' said the Prince. 'If it allows you to survive to the next session. Especially your second and third clauses. Wiseman will mobilise every possible voice in and out of Parliament, but especially in Ireland, will he not, Prime Minister? What you propose will virtually paralyse the hierarchy. It is ingenious, oh, most commendably so, but it will be represented as brutal persecution notably because it will upset the so-called Cardinal's financial plans. For example, we hear that he is incarcerating a Miss Talbot in a nunnery to lay his hands on her fortune of eighty thousand pounds. If clause two of the bill goes through, he won't be able to get his hands on it, will he?'

'No, Your Royal Highness. Your Royal Highness has, as usual, put your finger on the critical point. If the hierarchy can't touch any bequests of that kind, Wiseman might as well pack up and go back to Rome, we reckon.'

'What is this affair of this Miss Talbot, Albert? I have not been told.'

'I have only just heard of it myself, dearest. She is a young person of eighteen, a relative of Lord Shrewsbury, now our leading Catholic peer, who had her presented at court last year, so you have seen her, quite a pretty *Mädchen*, who has been confined in a convent and is being induced to become a nun there, whereupon her fortune, which derives from her deceased family, the Talbots, will, as nuns may not possess money, become the property of the Roman Church – that is, of Cardinal Wiseman. Her guardian is a priest, the Revd Dr Doyle, who has assumed the title of Bishop of Southwark. If the bill passes, Dr Wiseman can't receive her money. It is all being hushed up, and I am told not even Lord Truro knows about it, although the girl is a ward of Chancery. Such is Romanism, which we do not allow in Germany, though it happens there, I fear.'

'Really, Albert? The imprisoned heiress! It sounds like one of Mr Dickens's or Mr Wilkie Collins's novels. And who is to rescue her? Why, who but Lord John himself!'

And Her Majesty went into peals of royal laughter, in which the Prince joined moderately, while the Prime Minister smirked and shivered.

'But tell us, Prime Minister,' the Prince added soberly, 'do you have the necessary support in the House to pass this decisive measure against the Roman hierarchy?'

'Er . . . yes, Your Royal Highness, I think so.'

'You think so, *ach*? You think your majority will be sufficient?'

'I . . . er . . . the country is behind us, sir.'

'It is. But it does not vote in the House of Commons. How do you think the Irish Members will vote? For you, or against you?'

'Well . . . er.'

'The priests in Ireland do not like your bill, which will also deprive them of money and their titles, eh? And how will the Radicals vote? Mr Roebuck, for example?'

'Well, perhaps not Roebuck, but the Radicals have constituencies, and their supporters are mostly Protestants.'

'*Ach*, good. Mr Cobden, Mr Bright, who is a Quaker and dislikes all bishops whether Roman or Church of England, will vote for you? And the followers of our late friend, Sir Robert Peel, such as Mr Gladstone, they will vote for you?'

'Well, perhaps not Mr Gladstone, but . . .'

'With Mr Gladstone goes Sir James Graham and a dozen others, I fear! And the Conservatives, as the Tories call themselves now, the Protectionists, they will vote for you? Mr Disraeli, for example?'

'Well, perhaps not Mr Disraeli, but the Tories thirst for a revenge against those that insult Her Majesty . . .'

'But they also thirst for revenge against you Whigs and the Free Traders who have ruined them by taking taxes off their corn, isn't it? Will they not listen to Mr Disraeli when he finds reasons why they should postpone their revenge against the Pope when they can at once achieve their revenge against Free Trade by helping the Irish and Radicals and the tender conscience of Mr Gladstone to put you out?'

'Well, er . . .'

'Surely, Lord John, we are back to the point that I, that is Her Majesty and myself, have been making to you for months: your government is weak, the House is disloyal and unmanageable, and the only answer is to strengthen the executive?'

'I should welcome the adherence of any prominent figures who would bring additional support to my administration, Your Royal Highness, and I am in constant touch with those we might recruit, but . . .'

'We are thinking of Lord Aberdeen in the House of Lords, Prime Minister, and Clarendon in the Lower House, a true ministry of all the talents in this grave moment, all the talents – even including Mr Disraeli – and Mr Gladstone, who would then not wish to be left out . . . and . . .'

'But not Pilgerstein! We will not have Pilgerstein, Lord John!'

'Pilgerstein, Your Majesty? But who is Pil——'

'Palmerston, of course, Lord John. In reconstructing your ministry you will have the perfect opportunity to leave him and his insolence out of it. We would be happy with young Granville or someone like that – he is a Whig, isn't he? – at the Foreign Office, but we must get rid of Pilgerstein while we have a single friend left in the world! Why, the Emperor of Austria is hardly on speaking terms with me. Fancy inviting him here to see Prince Albert's Great Exhibition! Really!!!'

'Her Majesty feels *very* strongly about the studied insolence and insubordination of Lord Palmerston, and so do I!' The Prince chimed in. 'It is time you put your foot down – all three of us together . . .'

'He is popular in the country and . . .' murmured the Prime Minister.

'He is a menace to peace,' said Queen Victoria. 'I shouldn't wonder if he wanted to embroil us in war with the Pope. Your idea is so much better!'

'Actually, he strongly opposed any warlike move, Your Majesty. He said we couldn't fight any such war because . . .'

'Coward!' shouted the Queen, rising in a sudden fury. 'Coward and bully! All bullies are cowards. This is not a nation that accepts cowards. You must get rid of him. You have our leave to withdraw.'

'Thank you, Your Majesty, Your Royal Highness,' said the Prime Minister, backing into the icy blasts that swept the corridor outside.

14

Mr Delane had spent a genial Christmas with the family, had put in some enjoyable hunting, and had looked forward to the new year with considerable satisfaction. He had taken soundings at several dinners and receptions that preceded the full return of the *beau monde* from their country estates and from visits abroad; an outline of what the Government was going to do about the papal aggression was emerging, though the ministers, remembering that they were speaking to *The Times* when conversing (however informally) with Delane himself, were maintaining appropriate evasiveness about the Queen's speech, merely signifying by hints and winks that they had found a watertight 'formula'.

This was not wholly reassuring. Mr Delane had toyed with the idea of goading them with another magisterial leading article but decided for the moment to stand aside and give them a chance to speak for themselves, whereupon *The Times* would pronounce whether it met the just demands of the people of England, as already marshalled in previous leaders, or not. *The Times* at any rate was clearly speaking for England, and had unmistakably masterminded the campaign that must end in the humiliation of the Pope. Circulation had responded encouragingly.

It was evident that Lord John was basking in his undoubted popularity in the country. He looked well, everybody said, and in his occasional public appearances authoritative and self-confident; the word was that he was benefiting from a new medical treatment. This had been partly confirmed by remarks made by Mr Cam Hobhouse (now being considered for a peerage), who had it from Mr Thackeray, who swore such a treatment had saved his life a year previously and had in gratitude dedicated his novel *Pendennis* to Dr John Elliotson, its practitioner. Mr Delane frowned at the rumour that this was something to do with the disreputable fad known as animal magnetism, or mesmerism, on which *The Times* had yet not found occasion to pass final judgement, though *The Lancet* had done so and had condemned it.

Meanwhile the stream of petition and protest had diminished only as the pool of protest had been drained; it was still flowing and *The Times* gave it full coverage, as well as to any particularly bellicose and disloyal utterances from Ireland. Mr Delane had written to his correspondent in Rome to request background despatches on the papal mood and the continued deterioration of conditions in the papal states. He congratulated him on his warning that Asiatic influences prevailed on Italian attitudes in the south, and particularly in the Roman court, rendering them contemptuous of the slightest sign of weakness in negotiations of any sort so that, alike for English travellers dealing with officials or diplo-mats dealing with cardinals, the only method that would produce satisfactory results was to hit hard from the word go, to be unyielding in one's demands and to call in British force at the slightest sign of Italian, and specifically papal, prevarication. Such advice won admiring comment; from readers of *The Times*, they averred, let the British position be Palmerstonian.

What Mr Delane heard of the British response hardly seemed to meet this prescription, which really required re-course to Elizabethan enactments and penalties. Moreover, Mr Delane detected a weak-kneed tendency in liberal thought to confuse resistance to aggression with intolerance. Even his leaders had failed wholly to convince the public that the power of Catholicism was totally different in method and effect from that of any other religion. He bristled when he passed the Jesuit establishment in Down Street in his carriage or on horseback to the Row, or when he heard on good authority that when the Cardinal attended a dinner party the guests went down on their knees as he entered the room. He gave prominence to the report of his Rome correspondent that at a service to celebrate the submission of England to the Holy See, the newly converted Lords Beaumont and Feilding had made themselves conspicuous by the fervour of their prostrations.

Indecorous. Un-English.

It was disappointing therefore to hear Mr Cobden say in the Reform Club that the faith that primarily required de-fence was Free Trade, still menaced by the House of Lords and by Mr Disraeli's machinations in the Commons. Any coalition against the Pope that risked also producing a majority for the Corn Laws was anathema; the Pope's pre-tensions were inconsiderable, measured against mankind's true grail: universal free trade. That was the one thing to work for, whatever rituals a man might favour. That was the hope for universal peace, and in pursuit of it he would cease to spend another penny on the Navy and Army. . . . His friend

SELLING OFF!!

Punch, certain that Parliament would destroy
Wiseman's attempt to re-establish Catholicism, shows
how his regalia would be knocked down cheap to a
Jewish dealer in old clothes.

Mr Bright and Manchester generally would stand behind him in this.

Lord Ashley, on the other hand, told Mr Delane on the steps of the Athenaeum that God had called Lord John to frustrate the popish plot, and that whatever the High Church and dissent differed on, they were at one on this; while the school of Manchester economists, as enemies of the labouring classes, wishing to keep them in sweated ignorance to swell business profits, was little better, morally, than popery. 'And this I have told him, though, after his noble letter to the Bishop of Durham, it was hardly necessary,' he added.

Mr Delane added up the ayes and noes in the commons, and the *placets* and *non placets* in the Lords. The Duke of Norfolk was proposing to give Lord John his immensely weighty support in the Upper House, where old 'Pepper and Potatoes' was held in immense respect, particularly after he had condemned ultramontanism and the new hierarchy, and thus abrogated his position as the leading Catholic duke. One could undoubtedly look forward to as remarkable and practical a suggestion from him as he had produced back in the days of the potato famine when he had recommended the starving classes to relieve the pangs of hunger by adding a little pepper to their drinking water – which he said would prove almost as helpful a specific as a good dinner, and a good deal cheaper. With such an august and creative speaker to back him, Lord John could surely not lose in either House, and Mr Delane was reassured. The only question was, really, would the Government's bill go far enough?

Anything to keep the pot boiling while everyone waited for the opening of Parliament.

*　　*　　*

The House cheered him rather half-heartedly when Lord John entered, ready for the fray. Nevertheless, enough order-papers were waved to reassure him that those who glared in grim disapproval were in the minority. His plan was to survey broadly the whole field of battle, a Wellington marshalling arguments as if they were troops and batteries. This must be the fight of his career: the independence of Britain against the Catholic Church; the battles fought by Richard II, which Elizabeth, Cromwell and William III refought. At the despatch-box he squared his narrow shoulders; the sight of the tiny champion of Truth and Liberty brought a tear to Lady Russell's eye as she looked down from the gallery.

Fleetingly, he wished it was only a fight for franchise reform. . . .

He knew the first thing was to deal with those who were saying Rome was no more dangerous to the country than the Wesleyans: to smash Roebuck and forestall Bright who used such specious arguments. Next: to deepen the apprehensions of those who still doubted whether a mere dozen so-called bishops in suburban made-to-measure sees (even backed by the papacy's age-old cunning) could undermine the strongest country in Europe.

So he settled down to show them that against the weapons which the Pope deployed England was *not* the strongest: nothing like. Far stronger against Rome's barrage of bulls were France, Austria, Spain: Catholic lands that knew exactly what they were up against and whose governments insisted that they had the last word – *placet* or *non placet* – over any bull or ploy from Rome. As Britain herself, when she was Roman Catholic, had done, and he went through the long but illuminating history of praemunire again, as some MPs dozed off. . . . Britain was now the weakest country in Europe – weaker than autocratic Prussia and other Protestant countries. Weak because she was disarmed by a mild, liberal constitution, tolerant in religion, dedicated to free speech and equality before the law – all of which made her an easy target for subversion and infiltration. Hence the insulting language of Pope and Cardinal such as they would not dare to adopt elsewhere: and which was a calculated demonstration of impunity to open a campaign to assert papal power, to assert the secular meaning of infallibility, and to overawe the anglicised Catholic laity as a preliminary to overawing everybody else: in short, to develop temporal, not just spiritual, jurisdiction.

Examples, Mr Speaker? Ireland, where the tolerated Catholic bishops had, at their synod in Thurles, rejected Parliament's legislation to improve and fund schools on the ostensible grounds that such schools would be injurious to Catholic faith and morals. Similar interference even with the most sensitive handling of the education problem must now be anticipated in England (when the Government found time to reform education, of course). In Ireland, too, the Pope had long imposed a hierarchy with territorial titles, recognised simply out of courtesy by the English administration as part of its tolerant realism in governing a land where Catholics outnumbered Protestants by nine to one.

Having made Honourable Members' flesh creep over the pervasive power of popery and the implications of canon law where no limits were set to its expansion, he then, with the aid of the Attorney-General, turned to the remedies, first laying down the underlying liberal principle that penalties must be proportionate to the injury inflicted. A principle that ruled out the more extreme remedies which were in the past prescribed by anti-Catholic legislation, since these, while still technically in force, transgressed the spirit of the Emancipation Act of 1829: an act which the Pope and his cardinal had evidently studied with care with a view to staying marginally within the law.

Now the House sat up as Lord John announced that the bill would change the law. The injury inflicted to the Queen and the established Church was to be met by a fine of £100 on any clerics who assumed titles of any locality on the map of the kingdom, to be imposed only by the Attorney-General. This rule made the titles to the new sees null and void, and hence disposal of property or money to such clerics in breach of this extension of 10 Geo. IV (which had only prevented Roman Catholic bishops assuming titles of sees to which Anglican bishops were already appointed and did not touch

Birmingham or Beverley). With such territorial bishoprics now forbidden to them, Catholic bishops had perfect freedom to minister spiritually to their flocks, just as Wesleyan pastors did, but could not control funds, bequests or trusts on behalf of the Roman Church. Such monies would now pass to the Crown to dispose of. This being the source of its income under canon law, he claimed he had thus spiked the guns of the new hierarchy.

He sat down to modest applause. For four days Members of the House debated the proposals in exhaustive detail to see how, or if, they would work, and delved deep into the theology, ecclesiology, and indeed ecclesiolatry, of papal intentions. Rising in the small hours exhausted and irritated, and then, after a few hours of snatched sleep, they reported to their friends or associates in clubs, at evening parties, at church meetings, in chop-houses, in informal Cabinet discussions. The Irish members, strengthened by the support of the Earl of Arundel and Surrey, whose father the Duke of Norfolk had repudiated the hierarchy only to be himself repudiated by his more ultramontane son in the House of Commons, discussed tactics with the Cardinal over alcoholic refreshment in Golden Square.

In the end the House voted 395 to 63 for bringing in the bill.

However, the Cardinal was not down-hearted. 'The key to the situation is Ireland, my dear sons,' he told them. 'That is where they are soft; their consciences are tender there; they know that there we, the majority, Protestant or Catholic, are in rags, while they, the minority, go in purple and fine linen on our tithes and taxes, hogging the best places even in minor administrative posts. You do well to press this point, and you have the telling assistance of Friend Bright and the Radicals, the Manchester men whose ears are stuffed with cotton and care only for the Gospel according to Manchester. They will see the point about Ireland, and we are helped by protests, private as he imagines they are, from Lord Clarendon, the Lord Lieutenant, who thinks the fuss over whether he gave our bishops undue precedence at the castle is nothing compared with the risks Russell is running over an Irish civil war. The Irish press is making the point that the English are planning to despoil the Church in both islands as they did under Henry VIII, and the argument against applying the bill's provisions to the Church in Ireland as well as England is producing second thoughts. *The Times* is definitely uneasy. I am preaching in St John's Wood in aid of funds to erect a convent and schools for a thousand poor children and for a refuge for indigent female servants. Now, will they say I ought to be prevented from handling money given in charity by the laity for such a purpose? A large and respectable congregation which gives generously will talk about it. What Anglican bishop will they compare me with? Be of good cheer – God is on our side and He will deliver us.'

And Mr Delane was uneasy. He noted that Honourable Members on both sides of the House were not impressed by the bill. Mr John Walter, MP, of the family that owned *The Times*, gathered Members to meet him and tell him that those who voted for it found it somehow inadequate; while those who damned it had made it look pettish and paltry as well as penal and intolerant. Mr Delane talked to other influential persons as he progressed from dinner party to dinner party, and, disregarding the extremists led by Lord Winchilsea who wanted the Cardinal arraigned under praemunire and the English fleet patrolling the papal coasts, concluded that the measure was not as decisive and inspiring as befitted the scale of the outcry and protest of which he had made *The Times* the mouthpiece. He sniffed the political air and sensed widespread disappointment and anticlimax. Accordingly *The Times* passed judgement and pronounced itself unsatisfied: 'We cannot think the measure is adequate to what the emergency requires and the opinion of England demands. What is merely prohibiting titles and trust powers if we leave to the hierarchy the full power of synodical action and the ability to set the seal of infallibility on their decisions . . .?'

96

Just what such synodical action, operating penniless and under legal threat if it transgressed the new law, would do, *The Times* did not spell out, though it had called it a terrible threat to the nation in many leading articles, but left it to Lord John to think out further defences, since nobody else had put forward any better ideas except recourse to praemunire; while the Opposition's case for taking no action at all was supported by the assertion that any bill, besides being penal and therefore intolerant, was sure to be somehow evaded by the hierarchy's practised cunning developed over fifteen hundred years in handling princes and governments that rarely lasted more than fifteen or twenty.

In this atmosphere of doubt and hesitation, despite its huge majority in the House, the Cabinet was at sixes and sevens within days.

15

And Cardinal Wiseman was right.

Mr Benjamin Disraeli was thirsting to win office – to become a minister of the Crown. He had become leader, in the House of Commons, of his party, the Stupid, *alias* Tory, Party which was amazed to find a Hebrew as their leader. But they could field nobody else with a tenth of his brains, capacity for work, mastery of the arcane rules of the House – or a twentieth of his mordant ambition. When Sir Robert Peel, in a fright over the Irish famine, had betrayed the party and joined the Whigs, the Free Traders and the Manchester men to repeal the Corn Laws, Mr Disraeli had cut the apostate to bits with a wit and sarcasm that had produced tears and cheers in his demoralised and beheaded party. In consequence they had had to buy him an estate to disguise him as a country gentleman, as a Tory leader had to be. So lo and behold he was their leader in the Commons, though only leader of the Opposition because a score of Tories had crossed the floor with Sir Robert and were in the process of being absorbed into the Grand Whiggery led by little Sir John: not unlike the way in which Cardinal Wiseman was absorbing Puseyite Anglican clergymen who finally crossed the ecclesiastical floor to Rome.

'You see, my love,' Mr Disraeli was saying to his wife Mary Anne, whom he loved devotedly for her money which had got him into Parliament (but he was also very, very fond of her despite her eccentricities in dress and ignorance of the classics), 'we only lost by fourteen votes. We have only to get seven or eight more Members on our side to be able to turn Lord John out and form our own administration!' They were discussing the results of the debate on agricultural distress which Lord John had so ineptly given Disraeli the opportunity under the House rules to force on the Government by alluding to it in the Queen's speech.

'But could you really form an administration on so little?'

'On less, as a minority government, if they lost votes in the committee stages of this popery debate.'

'But what good. . . ?'

'What good, my love? We should have the initiative and it's everything in a parliamentary fight to have the initiative. We might even force a general election. We should be weak at first but we'd gather speed – all sorts of things might happen to fill our sails . . .'

'But Dizzy, my love, you wouldn't be prime minister, would you? Lord Stanley would be prime minister, surely? Or have I got it wrong again?'

'No, my dear. Stanley would be prime minister – at first. But I'm going to be prime minister in the end, you may count on it. Good evening, My Lord Duke! Mr Paxton, sir!'

An evening walk to the site of the Crystal Palace, to which the finishing touches were being added, had become a fashionable promenade for the nobility, gentry and respectable merchant class. Mr Disraeli had doffed his hat and bowed to the Duke of Devonshire, who was making his regular tour of inspection with Mr Paxton, and would have improved on the opportunity to embellish his expressions of esteem but for the fact that he observed that the Duke was making for the Queen and the Prince, who also were admiring the long prospect of iron and glass, close to which crates and packages containing the exhibits were beginning to pile up under guard by watchmen and police. Tactfully he steered Mrs Disraeli away; the Queen, he knew, still viewed him with suspicion as a dangerous demagogue; that would have to be changed in due time. . . .

The first signs of spring could be discerned on this mild afternoon: the birds were in song, the ducks were frolicking in the Serpentine, the grass was freshly green, the trees were almost in bud. Friends met and chatted in cordial groups, commenting on the grace and splendour of the huge edifice. Mr and Mrs Disraeli found they had, in turning, come nearly face to face with Cardinal Wiseman and his entourage, likewise tacking away from the path of royalty. For a second their eyes met; but the time had not come (if ever it did) for overt recognition on either side, however minimal; yet neither could be said, or to be observed by any passing gossip, to have cut the other. Technically they were at war; but had not had to come to close quarters and engage; and it might never come to that, events would define their social relationship, if they were destined to require one. Mr Disraeli always enjoyed the sensation of being recognised as a key figure in the great national game of destiny: for nearly twenty years now he had never been mistaken for some lesser person, or ignored by anybody of even the highest consequence. The Queen received him. How far he had come since he had worn an embroidered waistcoat to advertise himself – thanks to Mary Anne. But he saw to it that she was honoured by all – and some day. . . .

Three gentlemen, one in clerical attire, were strolling by the waterside, having reviewed the progress of the great glass bubble, which Mr Ruskin had contemptuously dismissed as a 'cucumber frame'.

'When it opens, my dear Patmore, you ought to write a

celebratory ode for *The Times*,' remarked the clergyman.

'Oh no, Charles,' replied the other, 'I can't do that sort of thing. Besides, isn't it Tennyson's job, Milnes? I mean he's the Laureate.'

'Of course it is,' said the third man. 'And he's taking it very seriously. But I haven't seen him lately. He's house-hunting – his wife is shortly going to give him the happiness of seeing his first-born . . .'

'A year ago one wouldn't have credited it,' said Coventry Patmore. 'The "Emperor" married! And he hardly knew if he was going to go on with it or back out, when he got ready for church! But it has worked! He's the happiest man alive, except for your humble servant! *I* am the happiest . . .'

'I dispute that,' laughed the cleric. '*I'm* the happiest, or, perhaps we should say that you and I are the joint two happiest men alive – but anyway it's a joy to recruit Alfred to the ranks of blissfully happy married men. Happiness in marriage, the total union of two souls, two bodies, is the fore-taste of heaven . . .'

'Yes, Charles,' broke in Mr Patmore excitedly. 'It signifies the intimate union of Christ and His Church, and is the mystical sacrament of earth and heaven and is fulfilled at that moment of ecstacy which is the joining point of time and eternity in the exchange of unutterable joy by husband and wife, bridegroom and bride. In my poem . . .'

'Yes, it is,' said the Revd Charles Kingsley. 'And it wipes away all sin and doubt and infidelity. It is a hermetic therapy. When poor Anthony Froude came to me in awful depression, thrown out by Oxford and by his family, and penniless, my wife and I brought her sister Charlotte Grenfell to Eversley in a similar state of desolation – only hers was even worse, for she had become a Catholic and decided to be a nun – and in a matter almost, I would say, of hours, they were in each other's arms and I married them well-nigh within days! Froude said to me afterwards: "This is really what I needed all the time and if I'd had Charlotte I'd never have written that damned book." He meant his novel *Nemesis* which the

Rector of Exeter publicly burned as paganist, you may recall. And as for Charlotte herself – she's never entered a papist church since. Marriage, she told me, and he confirmed it, was all the mystical truth a Christian needed. They were right, and I feel as if I had converted them from that dreadful religion which would have kept them forever from fulfilment. They go to bed, he told me, as one goes to holy communion – only, it lasts longer.'

'I hope such happiness may await me,' said Mr Milnes. 'I may as well tell you, I am engaged to be married myself.'

The others exclaimed their congratulations and Patmore added: 'Dare one ask? Is it to be the lovely Miss Nightingale, whose name has not infrequently been mentioned with your own?'

'Er . . . well, no,' said Mr Milnes. 'There was a great friendship, and I asked for her hand on several occasions, we seemed so close. But frankly, I was just not good enough for her. No, my friends, I mean it. Miss Nightingale has some high destiny that precludes matrimony. Among her friends is Archdeacon Manning, who it seems certain will go over to Rome, and perhaps she will follow him. She has heard voices which come from God! If Manning becomes her spiritual guide, she may end as one of their saints, I do believe. I tell you this in confidence, for it would be awful if people thought I had trifled with her affections. No! No! It is over, at her wish. I have seen her at several receptions this season, I saw her again last night, but hardly spoke. It wouldn't be suitable for me to be seen speaking to her now. I am happy to be affianced to Miss Annabel Crewe – you must know the Crewe connection? Lord Crewe has long been a friend of mine. Ah, good afternoon, dear Mrs Norton. . . .'

The other two gentlemen doffed their hats to the ladies who had been courteously intercepted by Mr Milnes, and who had met the famous authoress on previous occasions, and therefore knew of her unhappy circumstances: a loveless marriage to a brutal husband who deprived her of her children, kept her money, had accused her of having had an affair with Lord Melbourne at No. 10 Downing Street, dragged her into court where he lost his case, and defied with contempt and impunity the disapproval of society for his all-too-well-known tyrannies.

But she was so charming, so beautiful, and so generally received in the best society, that it was easy to forget the dark shadow which fell across her life. So that, when she asked them what, other than the Crystal Palace, they had been so earnestly discussing, the Revd Charles incautiously replied, 'We were congratulating Mr Milnes on his approaching nuptuals.'

'Ah, my dear bird of paradox – how typical of you! I congratulate *you*, in my turn,' said the Hon. Mrs Norton with the most disarming smile, looking up from lowered eyelids in that entrancing way she had. 'Happy man, acquiring a slave to attend you and a portion no doubt to add to your assets? I have to confess that I can never *quite* extend my felicitations to the young lady in such a case, however much in love she thinks she is, or even in fact *is*. But you know me, dear Mr Milnes.'

'I understand your feelings, dear Mrs Norton,' replied Mr Milnes, as it were for them all. 'I can but assure you that the mistress of Fryston Hall shall be no slave, but as free a creature as ever trod this earth.'

'I know what you mean, which is you mean well,' said Mrs Norton, laughing. 'The fact remains that I count no married woman free in this country except one – the Queen herself. What she has is hers of absolute right, for she is above the law of England. Do you know, I intend to write her a letter, without getting my husband's permission, to appraise her of her privilege, not an iota of which is extended by the law to one half of her subjects. If I print it as a pamphlet, of course, my husband will exact from me the last ha'penny of my royalties, as is his right in law. And if he disagrees with what he reads, he is within his right to thrash me. And now I must hurry on. I have a rendezvous with the dear Duke of Devonshire and his architect,

Mr Paxton, who are going to show me round and explain the principles of this amazing structure.'

Followed by her duenna she left them, hats in hands, looking deflated.

'A shocking story of a marriage, poor Mrs Norton's,' said the Revd Charles Kingsley with a heavy sigh. 'He still deprives her of her children, and one remembers how he reduced her to hysteria in the court case. Such a marriage calls to mind the old proverb, "*Corruptio optimi pessima est.*"'

16

She spoke in a low voice, her cheeks burning, her eyes fixed on the floor of his drawing-room, which he used for consultations with his lady patients.

'I am obsessed with him, Doctor. I refused to marry him and my parents were furious. He is highly eligible, well connected, a Member of Parliament, a poet and author. I think he loved me and was very disappointed. But I knew we were not suited. I have something to do, I don't know what it is, but I know I can't marry. If not him, then nobody! But I can't stop thinking about him, and it's the season, I meet him everywhere, I mean at all the big affairs, the receptions, the routs – you understand. I met him again a few nights ago. As usual, he hardly spoke to me, a mere bow as on other occasions. As you say, you saw me on one such. But I expected him to speak! I wanted to find him longing to talk to me, willing to give me another opportunity....' Her voice faded.

The doctor prompted her gently: 'To change your mind, to accept him?'

'Yes. No! To refuse him again, I am sure. Oh, God help me ... I have prayed! To keep open another decision anyway. For him to show me his sympathy. He didn't. I had killed it in him, perhaps. He didn't show indifference but a marked avoidance. There was no acknowledgement of our friendship, no confidence such as I felt for him.... I felt most horribly wounded – how could he speak to me like an ordinary acquaintance? I have learned the reason, he's engaged to somebody else ... I am in agony, I cannot bear it. I cannot bear to be so ... rejected – abandoned. I could have done so much for him. Oh dear....'

She was near to tears, but she did not break down.

'It is a terrible time for you, but you know you will get over it, Miss Nightingale. You know you must put the whole past, all your dearest memories behind you. Others have, you know that...'

'I thought I could do that when I first refused him. I could not, he was in all my dreams ... waking as well as in sleep. I am fearful it will go on. Oh yes, since I last saw him I have dropped into reveries about him.... I am weak, weak, weak! I cannot go on with this life, all this society chitter-chatter, and relapsing from it just to think of him, of ... of men.... I am useless like all the silly women I chitter-chatter with. I think sometimes I'll kill myself...'

'I have to tell you that you must think of no such wicked thing, you who are young, so beautiful, with the best part of your life before you ...'

'Chitter-chatter, tea with old maids as another old maid! Why has God made women like this? Not wanted by anybody – not wanted for anything?'

'What do you think I can do for you? You are a lady, you have to live the life of a lady.' He moved a little closer. 'There are things you can do – charities, for instance.'

'You gave me your card. I asked about you. You do help people. You have powers. Mesmerism ... magnetism. Can you help me to stop these useless dreams, this hankering.... Until that is burned out of me I shall not find a way...'

'Yes, Miss Nightingale, I can perhaps help you. You have immense powers in yourself. I am not sure if you can let me help you. The therapy I use does help some patients.

THIS IS THE BOY WHO CHALKED UP "NO POPERY!"— AND THEN RAN AWAY!!

...ord John Russell as a street-urchin who has scrawled
...o Popery' on Cardinal Wiseman's door, then
...un away.

Others I can't influence at all. I can only try. Would you like me to – here, now, no hesitations?'

'Try,' she whispered. 'In God's name, try.'

'Look me in the eye then, and yield yourself. Tell yourself this is something you must do, despite yourself. This is a battlefield in which to win victory you must first surrender....'

Dr Ashburner saw the struggle within Miss Florence Nightingale. He made slow passes in almost silence. The clock ticked, the carriages rumbled in Grosvenor Street. Part of her was trying, if clumsily, not like poor Mrs Carlyle who had fought him all the way... and successfully resisted, though she was certainly the type. Then he sensed his patient was letting go. Abandoning the ramparts of that ferocious will. Yielding. Letting him into her.

'What is your name?' His voice was gentle but authoritative.

'Florence. Flo.'

'And this man's name?'

'Mr Monckton Milnes.'

'Florence, he is not for you. When you wake up, you will have forgotten him, you won't think of him. If you see him, you will try politely not to meet him. If you cannot avoid meeting him, you will treat him casually as a rather uninteresting stranger. Your mind will be on other things. You have work to do. What is that work? What do you feel you could do, what do you *want* to do, Florence?'

'I want to be a nurse, working in a hospital.'

'A nurse! In a hospital! What can you be thinking of? A delicately nurtured lady like you? You cannot conceive of the filth of a hospital, the horrible disgusting sights, the language, the screams, the blood, the pus, the stench of a public hospital. You could not stand it an hour! I must earnestly tell you to put any such idea out of your mind. You will not think about it after I have wakened you. Wake up, Miss Nightingale!'

17

'My dearest, I am sure everything is going to be all right. We won the debate, hands down! My levee was a complete success. All your colleagues were full of praise for your speech. Everyone I spoke to complimented you. Wiseman is said to be practically packing up to go back to Rome. I wish Dizzy would go with him and take the first boat to Jerusalem! But he was beaten too. . . .'

The Prime Minister pushed his half-eaten egg aside peevishly. Fanny was spoiling his breakfast and *The Times* and the *Morning Chronicle*, Charles Dickens's paper, the *Daily News*, would be against him too, he felt certain. Surely in Downing Street he could be left alone for an hour?

'No, he wasn't beaten, Fanny. He lost by only fourteen votes. That is a big success for the Protectionists. I could hardly believe it . . .'

'But he didn't turn you out, my love, did he? And that is what he wanted.'

'He still does. What he has shown is that the House is not really behind me. Surely you can see that. I beat him by 281 to 267. That's 541 votes in all. He lost by only fourteen, a year ago he lost by twenty-one. With his help I got my anti-Pope bill by 395 to sixty-three. That's 458 votes in all. It tells me that the House is considerably more interested in Protection than in Wiseman. More excited in giving Dizzy a good run for his money than in showing that it realises that the Ecclesiastical Titles Bill is the paramount issue before it and before the country. The lesson of the way the House votes is what really matters.'

'But, my love . . .'

'And Wood has made things worse still with his budget . . .'

'But there's been no vote on that yet.'

'No, no, and there won't be. Yet! But the House hates the budget. Hates it. With a surplus of two and a half million

pounds and business booming, all he can propose is to reduce the national debt! Of course that may be the honest
course. And tax houses instead of windows. And fiddle around
taking the tax off soap or paying for asylums for lunatics.
Anything except see from the debate on Dizzy's motion, if
he couldn't read it in the papers, that what the public wants
is the abolition of the income tax! Where's that blessed bell?
Bring me some fresh coffee – and another cup for Lady
Russell. So – we plainly have it in our power to do it, and
we don't do it. Does that win us friends in the House? Or
does it leave people feeling we've cheated them of what is
theirs and what we owe them? Wood tells the House, oh
yes, it's an iniquitous tax and we shall abolish it sooner or
later. But now is the time. I need a big success now – now!
What do they really care about Wiseman when we withhold
their money? Eh? They can see that if we don't do it now,
some ghastly thing will happen, like another famine or a
war and the chance will be lost. Why, there's going to be a
war with the Cape Kaffirs anyway and the Cape colonists
don't want to pay for it . . .'

'A just war. As a war with the Pope would be! Surely the House
cannot be so blind to all morality to put a paltry tax before. . . .
And anyway, why didn't you tell the Chancellor all this first?'

'I've no head for figures. I fell asleep. Like Dr Ashburner's
watch-chain – tic-toc, tic-toc. But business men don't – figures
wake them up. They think of their profits. Profits, Cobden
tells them, are holy, and wants the Army disbanded and the
Navy laid up. And income tax abolished! And I need Cobden's
vote against Wiseman! Don't you see? More coffee? No, you'd
better go, dear. I've got Grey coming to see me in a minute.
He's going to threaten to resign if I decide not to enforce
the Ecclesiastical Titles Bill in Ireland . . .'

'But you wouldn't do that – I mean you will, won't you?
We can't treat Ireland differently from England. . . . Even
the Queen sees that . . .'

'If I don't somehow exclude Ireland from the bill, it's
Clarendon who will resign. You should see the despatches

I'm getting from him. But who else could keep Ireland quiet? Baring is shaky about it and I fear that others in the Cabinet have got cold feet since the House has shown its teeth.'

Lady Russell rose. 'You will manage, dear. There is nobody else but you. If it was you who threatened to resign, they'd all fall into line. The Empire depends on you. And the bishops. Why, you appointed most of them yourself! Wilberforce, Sumner, Musgrave, Short, Hinds, and, oh, I forget them all. Don't tell me Lord Palmerston could take over – he said such nice things about you to me at our assembly. . . . No, you cannot think of resigning. I couldn't bear it . . .'

'Then let us hope it won't come to that, my dear.'

*   *   *

But it did.

Broughams and carriages rumbled up to Downing Street. The summons to a Cabinet meeting was unexpected. True, the Government had been humiliatingly beaten in the division the previous night, but that had not seemed so very significant: the Premier had passed it off lightly with a shrug. Mr Locke King had proposed a modest reform of the franchise, a proposal not only that he had made before, but which Lord John had also made before and had opposed that evening only on the ground that he had already pledged himself to bring in a government measure, and a more far-reaching one, in the next session. Mr Locke King's motion was merely ill-timed. Admittedly Lord John's opposition to Mr Locke King did look as if Lord John regarded parliamentary reform as a personal monopoly of Lord John Russell's, and Locke King's motion as a personal insult.

Locke King, a typical radical gadfly, was only slipping his oar in to make an impression and to suggest that the time allotted to the Papal Aggression Bill was excessive and unwarrantedly ignored more pressing issues. It was cheeky of him and the Premier had firmly if a little pettishly put him in his place, counting doubtless on the Tories to help

him do so, since they had no liking for parliamentary reform in any guise, especially as Lord John had made no
secret of his intention eventually to reform the House of
Lords as well as the House of Commons by instituting a
system of life peerages, after papal aggression had been
disposed of. To show his commitment to this sacrilegious
intention, he had even offered such a life peerage to the
theologian Dr Lushington in advance, an offer that upset
the Queen as much as it did the hereditary peerage. Luckily
Dr Lushington had declined the honour.

But the Tories had vanished from their places and Locke
King had won, by a hundred votes to forty-six, for a modest
proposal to equalise the franchise as between the counties
(which voted, on pain of losing their jobs, for the younger
sons of lords) and the towns (which voted for radical MPs
like Mr Roebuck and Mr Locke King).

A nominal victory, in a thin House, arranged of course by wily
Mr Disraeli on purpose to engineer some sort of ministerial crisis.

Hence there was no obligation to take it as anything but
a smack in the face with a wet kipper, such as prime ministers were expected to take in good part from time to time . . .
so why the emergency Cabinet?

But there they were taking their usual places round the
table – Lord Grey, Lord Truro, Sir Charles Wood, Sir Francis
Baring, Mr Hobhouse (who had just become Lord Broughton),
and Messrs Labouchere and Fox Moule. Lord Carlisle was
in the City, Lord Lansdowne had gout, Lord Minto practically never attended Cabinet meetings anyhow and Lord
Palmerston was late as usual, but he was sure to lounge in
presently from the Foreign Office across the road.

'My Lords, Gentlemen,' said the Premier surveying the
small group round the table, 'I have a very serious matter
to raise with you today. As you know, I gave notice that I
would bring in a parliamentary reform bill in the next session.
A majority voted last night against my policy not to bring
one in this session. This amounts to a vote of no confidence
in the Government. It cannot be waved away. He glowered

for a moment at the Chancellor of the Exchequer, who looked sheepish. 'It is clear also that the budget is not acceptable to the public, the City or the House. You will, I imagine, have read *The Economist* this morning. I cannot go on. I have sent a message to the Queen requesting her to see me as a matter of urgency, and I shall place our seals of office at her disposal. Any other business? No? Yes, Lord Grey?'

'But, Prime Minister, what about Wiseman,' moaned Lord Grey.

'That is for the incoming government to decide. I have done my best. The country is solidly behind me, but I have not had the necessary support in the House. I cannot go on. It is out of my hands now.' A deep sigh, partly of relief, but mostly of despair, was to be heard. 'No other business. Then, good-morning.'

Lord John rose, bowed to them, drew himself to his full height (inclusive of his built-up boots) and walked out, just as Lord Palmerston walked in.

'We're out, eh?' said the Foreign Secretary cheerfully. 'My wife said we would be at breakfast. I wonder how they'll take it at the palace.'

'I doubt if they will send for you, anyway,' said the Chancellor of the Exchequer cattily. *He* thought it was a good, a *moral* budget, which was why he had not told them much about it in advance.

'Not yet,' said the outrageous Pam. 'Maybe you, Truro. Better get some practice in stamping on cardinals' hats,' he chuckled, and, lighting a cigar most illegally, strolled out.

18

'Crisis! Government out! Crisis! Read orl abaht it!' shouted the newsboys.

*

'To bring back the old Cabinet would be a despicable

intrigue,' thundered *The Times.* 'It fell on a budget which everyone condemned and a papal bill which no one approved. We require a new administration more capable of making Lord John Russell's principles work. The late ministry was too much of a coterie, and we need a wider range of character and powers than are to be found in a domestic circle.'

*

'Which is not to be found in this tattered so-called Parliament. Our prayers have been answered! Let us go to my private chapel and give thanks,' said Cardinal Wiseman, beaming at his household, as he threw down *The Times.*

*

'What did I tell you, my love?' cried Mr Disraeli before Mrs Disraeli had time to appear downstairs. 'We're in. The Queen has to send for Stanley. I'm off to see him now. I must give him the necessary backbone. It's a risk, but he must take it.'

*

'But I told you *not* to! You've lost your nerve, John,' shouted Lady Russell. 'Yes, I know you had a bad night. If Dr Ashburner had been able to come and magnetise you, you'd still be prime minister.'

The former prime minister put on his smoking-cap and looked for a book in the bookshelves. 'What though the day be lost? All is not lost. Far from it,' he muttered as Lady Russell flounced out.

*

'The Whigs out? Lord Lansdowne out? Then bang goes my school inspectorship job he'd promised me! We can't live on my poetry. Lansdowne can't keep me on as his secretary – it's a sinecure as it is! Your father will never let us get married now!' cried Mr Matthew Arnold to Miss Lucy Wightman, wringing his hands. 'And I do love you so, and need you so desperately!'

112

* * *

'Lord Stanley is a charming man,' said the Queen to her husband. 'He was an utterly *liebenswürdiger Mensch* at dinner last night. His poor old father is failing. He'll be Lord Derby any day now. He had no idea what was going to happen. But couldn't he keep things together for a bit, Albert? What do you think, my love? Anyway it's the proper thing to ask him to try, *nicht wahr?* The Queen's government must be carried on. I shall remind him of that.'

'Of course, *Liebchen*. He must try, and then report back to you. But it would mean Mr Disraeli leading in the Commons, you do realise that?'

'*Shrecklich!*' said the Queen, making a face.

'I think *unser* Dizzy is responsible for the whole crisis,' said the Prince. 'This plan of his to subsidise the farmers and property owners out of taxes as a dodge for not actually reimposing the Corn Laws will deceive nobody – just protection under another name. Not that I think he gives tuppence for protection. Far too clever. He merely pretends he's a Protectionist to keep the Tory Party together.'

'Then what is he really after, Albert?' said the Queen, smacking one of the dogs who was being impertinent with his nose.

'He wants to be prime minister, Victoria, *Glaube mir.*'

'Never!' cried the Queen. 'I would not have him. Never!'

The Prince looked harassed. 'Suppose the Tories came in as a minority government, put forward the Jew's foolish bill, were defeated on it by the Free Traders, and then asked us – you, that is – for a dissolution? I can see a very big row. Like in '48. The Chartists – they are not all in prison yet, you know. *Unsere polizisten sind zu freundlich mit dieser Kanaille.* The outcry against dear bread would be very violent. I have talked with respectable tradespeople who still fear a revolution. There's this German agitator, Engels, and those articles in the *Morning Chronicle* about starving tailors and seamstresses by this statist, Mr Henry Mayhew – oh, a lot of explosive material lying about.' He paused as the Queen

113

shook her head sadly, and added piteously, 'And what would happen, *Liebchen*, in an English revolution, to my Great Exhibition dedicated to world peace...? Unless we got it over with first... it opens in six weeks....'

Lord Stanley was announced.

'It is good, even if unexpected, to see you again so soon, Lord Stanley,' said the Queen. 'I am sure you know why we have sent for you? Are you prepared to try to form a government? My government must be carried on.'

'I am of course deeply honoured by Your Majesty's trust,' said the noble lord. 'I did assume you would make some such request. But Your Majesty will be aware that my party is in a minority in the House of Commons.' He gazed despairingly at the Prince, who nodded understandingly but made no comment. 'And in addition to that, I have almost nobody in that House fit to take up a minister's post, to... to understand how a department of state works. The ones who did are, ahem, all on the other side of the House now. I can think of only one....' He paused.

The Queen frowned. The Prince had the aspect of an iceberg. There was a silence. Lord Stanley shifted his weight from one leg to the other. He wished he was in the country, coursing hares... it could hardly be colder than the palace.

'That is *very* inconvenient,' said the Queen at last. 'I feel sure such a situation has never arisen before. It should not have happened, Lord Stanley. You could have foreseen eventualities and corrected the administrative shortcomings of your party. The constitution requires that the Opposition should always be competent to form a government, if only for a short time. The Queen's government must be carried on.'

'I believe,' remarked the Prince, 'that when Mr Pitt formed his first government at the sovereign's request late in the last century, he was unable to secure any support in the House of Commons and, as a temporary expedient, retained all the offices of state in the Commons himself.'

'On that precedent, Your Royal Highness,' said Lord Stanley, 'I should have to invest most of the major offices of state in that single talented member of the House of Commons, to whom I adverted——'

'We think we know the talented gentleman,' said the Queen, 'and great as his talents may be, and difficult, even unprecedented as the situation is, we cannot imagine that such a recourse would serve us in this century. Now, if you are unable to supply us with a government, what combination of talents in the rest of the House might, in your view, do so, pray?'

'I suggest Your Majesty tries to get the outgoing ministry to abandon so much of the papal bill that the followers of the late Sir Robert Peel can recombine with them. In other words, get Lord John Russell to do a deal with Lord Aberdeen and Sir James Graham. Like Lord John, both are men of inflexible moral principles...'

'We have suggested that to Lord John some time ago,' said the Prince.

'I can only advise you to try again,' said Lord Stanley glumly.

'And can *you* try again?' asked the Queen.

'I shall try, on the basis that Your Majesty's government must be carried on, and nobody else will do it, but first I must be sure that they can't or won't. I'll tell you what: I'll ask Gladstone, who should be back in town in a couple of days, if he would join me,' said Lord Stanley. 'He is also a man of inflexible principles. But I can at least find out what they happen to be, at the present juncture.'

On that undertaking they let him go.

*   *   *

'He just wouldn't, said he couldn't, the idiot,' said Mr Disraeli to his wife, striding up and down the drawing-room. 'When Russell told the House that Stanley had said to him that he was not in a position to form an administration, I corrected him. I insisted that the word 'now' be inserted in that statement. The leaves it open to him to try again if Russell can't reconstruct the Government. But everybody thinks I was rude to dear Lord John, and I'm in the doghouse with both parties. Not the gentleman. Pushy Jewboy.'

'Darling, darling, don't take it so to heart,' said Mrs Dizzy, clasping her husband to her bosom. 'You've been through it before and come up smiling. They're jealous, that's all. You're the only one who knows how to manage Parliament. There, there.'

19

Three Right Honourable Gentlemen, of inflexible moral principles, were closeted in the library in Chesham Place to discover if they could find a *modus vivendi* on which to join in order to carry on the Queen's government. She had laid this task on them personally, had urged them to leave no stone unturned and to spend as long as was necessary, giving a general effect of knocking their heads together and leaving them to it; and they felt obliged to do their utmost to meet her wishes.

To get the coach of the Queen's government back on the road, they had assured her that there was nothing they would shrink from doing, except compromise their personal honour or betray their moral principles.

There were statesmen in England in those days.

Even so, they were not sanguine about the outcome. They made notes of their talks, mainly with a view to explaining to Parliament, in lofty periods, why they had failed to come to any agreement from difficulties which reflected the highest credit on their own reputations.

They were Lord John Russell, the outgoing prime minister, who had convened them at his home after seeing the Queen in an impatient mood at Buckingham Palace, the Earl of Aberdeen, who had not been prime minister yet, but (though of course he did not know it) was doomed to become prime minister in a couple of years' time, and Sir James Graham, Baronet, who, a lot of people were wondering, in the complexities of the situation, if he *could* become prime minister,

THE KIDNAPPER.—A CASE FOR THE POLICE.

Kidnapper. "There's a Be-autiful Veil!!! Give me your Parcel, my Dear, while you put it on."

Catholic priest tries to cheat a small girl of her bag
sterling goodies by offering her a nun's pretty veil
exchange.

given his total inability ever to come to any decision on anything. They represented the Whig Party and that section of the Tory Party, known as 'Peelites', which together commanded enough votes in the House of Commons to give the Queen what she wanted.

They agreed on many things, and most of the things on which they did not agree in every particular could be adjusted without compromising their honour or principles.

'So, no truck with Protectionism, no Army and Navy cuts, another look at the possibility of abolishing the income tax, support for the Deceased Wife's Sister's Marriage Bill in defiance of most of the bishops' objections – we agree pretty well,' said Lord John. 'Now we come to the Ecclesiastical Titles Assumption Bill which both Houses of Parliament gave my late administration leave to introduce.'

'I can't see how we can get round that, Lord John. You know we are both against it and have said so publicly,' said Sir James, his lips compressed into a thin line. 'To satisfy me and Lord Aberdeen, it must be withdrawn.'

'But you both agree, and have said publicly, that the Pope's bull and the Cardinal's pastoral address were highly insulting to the Queen personally and defiant of our national sovereignty in general, and you both know she was absolutely beside herself with rage when she first had them read out to her – by the Prince, I believe. She was only a little calmer when I adverted to them in my usual audience in October.'

'Well, yes, we agree it was diplomatically unacceptable,' said the Earl. 'Bad show, very.'

'But we don't agree with what you want to do about it,' said Sir James.

'She thinks the No Popery demonstrations went too far,' said Lord Aberdeen. 'The Prince told me so. After all, she is Queen of the Irish, you know, as well as the English Catholics, and she remembers the wonderful reception she got in Ireland on her last visit. She couldn't go again if your bill became law, she'd be assassinated. And these attempts on her life in London itself have shaken her, brave gal as she is.'

'I believe we could make changes in it which would enable you to reconsider your position on it,' said Lord John.

The Earl and the Baronet looked interrogative.

'I think we could perhaps drop application of the entire bill from Ireland. We realise special problems attach to enforcing it in Ireland – over the ordination of priests and, er, that sort of thing.'

'It was madness to try to ram it down Irish throats,' said Sir James. 'You'd have had to drop that in any case.'

'So far, so good,' said the Earl. 'And. . . ?'

'I think we could drop the entire second and third clauses in respect of England and of course Scotland, as well as Ireland,' said Sir John. 'You object to penal legislation. So there wouldn't be any. They could appoint bishops and give them territorial sees in the way they want, and indeed have, and when they induced their subjects to make deathbed wills in their favour by witholding the sacraments it would be perfectly legal and they could operate and take over trusts, and all that, just as they do in any other Catholic – I mean, in any Catholic country.' There was perhaps a certain acerbity in his tone as he abandoned this provision.

'That is certainly coming a very long way. Very handsome,' said the Earl. 'So this would, you think, remove our difficulties about penal legislation against Catholics?'

'Ah, but it don't,' said Sir James. 'The first clause, which you wish to keep, imposes a fine of a hundred pounds on Catholic clerics who take titles attached to territorial sees. That's penal and discriminatory. We can't go along with it.'

'But the clause provides that only the Attorney-General can impose the fine,' said Sir John. 'Which he won't do. So no penalty.'

'Yes, but the bill would in effect be singling them out for censure publicly and thus treat them differently from the other religions practised in this country. That's discriminatory and so intolerant. We could not accept that,' said Sir James.

'Surely the immense surge of protest at their behaviour by the public, not to mention the extraordinary unanimity of the bishops on the matter, requires some acknowledgement?'

'Well, er . . .' said the Earl.

'I think I cannot make any further concessions,' said Lord John. 'My party, in the response to the Queen's speech, promised to make some answer to the papal aggression. We cannot honourably go back on that totally.'

'Then I am afraid we cannot connect ourselves with a policy which makes us party, in however small a degree, to your entire crusade against the Catholic religion and in effect would condone the deplorable outburst of bigotry which has disfigured the land,' said Sir James.

Lord John rose. 'I shall convey our regrets to the Queen,' he said. 'I note you do not expect us actually to apologise to the Pope.'

'That is the only concession we could make to you,' said Sir James. 'It is a large one, and I am not sure if we ought to go that far.'

*　　*　　*

A message was waiting for Mr Gladstone as the boat-train pulled into London Bridge terminus. Would he be so good as to call on Lord Stanley as a matter of urgency on his arrival? His Lordship's carriage was at Mr Gladstone's disposal and was waiting. The noble Earl apologised profusely for so precipitate an approach, but a matter of public importance was concerned.

Mr Gladstone smiled silkily and let himself be ushered to His Lordship's crested coach, have his knees covered by a plaid, and off they clattered to St James's Square.

Lord Stanley soon found that Mr Gladstone was fully seized of the details of the ministerial crisis.

'Somehow or other the Queen's government must be carried on, dash it. And if I have to rescue it, I've got to have some help from somebody. If you led the House and Disraeli took the Exchequer, both our parties would have to cobble up some sort of majority in the Commons, eh? We could see how we got on, as, well, as time went on.'

'I certainly agree with Your Lordship's statement that the Queen's government must be carried on,' replied Mr Gladstone. 'But to achieve that much to be wished for consummation by an arrangement which would appear to be the reconstitution of the late Sir Robert Peel's former administration, without removing the cause of its original dissolution, would seem to me an event little short of the miraculous raising of Lazarus from the tomb,' said Mr Gladstone. 'We have not the power of overriding nature which was then demonstrated by an Agency far beyond even the House of Commons to wield in this emergency.'

'No go, eh?' said Lord Stanley. 'Poor old Ben. He did *so* hope we could come in somehow. I'll tell the Queen.'

Mr Gladstone accepted His Lordship's kind offer to make use of his coach to complete his journey to Carlton House Terrace.

*   *   *

'So you see, they're all hopeless,' said the Queen 'Whatever shall we do?'

She had to repeat this remark twice before the Duke could catch it. He had been asked to sit, and had firmly but politely declined to avail himself of such an unheard-of breach of standing orders. He stood stiffly, as if on parade.

But when at last he had taken in the royal request he rose to the occasion, just as, a week previously, standing just as stiffly, he had proposed putting sparrow hawks into the Crystal Palace to keep out the sparrows who were nesting there.

'Is Your Majesty satisfied with Your Majesty's outgoing ministers?'

The Queen looked at the Prince and the Prince nodded to the Queen, who took a deep breath, gulped, and said (twice), 'Yes, er . . . yes, Duke.'

'Then I should advise Your Majesty to hang on to 'em.'

121

*   *   *

Crisis over – bar the shouting, which took days and days in the House and in the newspapers and wherever the nobility and gentry forgathered for convivialities.

And peace returned to Chesham Place. 'I told you, John, you had only to threaten to resign and they'd come running,' said Lady Russell, and kissed the top of the little man's head.

20

Mr Delane had scooped the resignation, of which he had heard at a party at Lady Granville's – and to which no other editor had an entrée; but he was now very worried. A government resignation was no part of *The Times*'s policy. *The Times* had criticised Lord John's anti-papal bill as inadequate, but all the talk now was of further surrenders. Indeed the only terms on which Lord John could have strengthened the Government team was to abandon the bill totally and to admit that Wiseman had won hands down. While the toings and froings between the palace and ministers and would-be ministers had gone on, *The Times*'s line had been to call for stronger men and stronger measures; but it looked as if the price of stronger men was weaker measures. Whatever the Duke proposed, it looked as if the same feeble Whig family coterie would return with even feebler measures.

One possible solution, to suggest that Lord Palmerston, the nation's favourite by far, should form a reconstructed government, was put forward by nobody but Lady Palmerston, who called on Lady Russell to accuse her of blocking it. Lady Russell had laughed in Lady Palmerston's face at the notion that her husband could have dared to recommend Lord Pilgerstein to the Queen as a successor to himself – whereafter Lady Pam referred to Lady Russell in public as 'Deadly Nightshade'.

Mr Delane inevitably heard of this tiff and very properly took Lady Russell's view and never mentioned the claims of the victor of Greece in *The Times*'s otherwise exhaustive examination of the permutations and combinations of political talent. He knew that, apart from all the other causes of friction between the Foreign Office and the palace, including the *Civis Romanus Sum* speech over Slesvig and Holstein, the Foreign Secretary was opposing Prussian ambitions just as the Queen was revolving in her mind an advantageous match between her first-born, the beloved Princess Vicky, now ten years old, and the heir to Prussia's throne.

Better than the return of an even weaker Russell ministry would have been for Stanley to come in with an even weaker government dedicated to Protectionism, as Dizzy wanted; *The Times* could then have led a blistering campaign to throw them out again and attention would have been diverted from the humiliations of the anti-papal campaign. But Mr Delane had found, from dropping in on Tory evening convivialities, that half the Tories had abandoned their faith in their own official policy; trouncing it would be flogging a dead horse – which was why Stanley had made only a show of trying to form a government.

So he had marked time by denouncing everybody's position as these were put forward as explanations for doing nothing, and the vast waste of time involved. Sarcastic leaders reduced Lord Aberdeen's and Sir James Graham's explanations to the argument that the nation was bound to submit to all the unreasonable and unfounded claims of the entrenched Roman Catholic hierarchy as these were successively adumbrated by synodical decisions and appeals to canon law overriding all parliamentary enactment on the plea that not to submit would be bigoted and intolerant on the Protestant side.

The mutilated bill was presented to the people as the redemption of the Government's pledges, and at last Mr Delane's leader writers could be briefed how to judge it. 'It is actually determined to strike out of the bill, which gave so poor and inadequate expression to public feeling, the second clause which renders invalid all deeds executed under the prohibited style and title, and the third clause by which all property left or conveyed to persons bearing these illegal titles is forfeited to the Crown.'

The result could not be clearer. 'It is unlawful for Dr Wiseman to call himself Archbishop of Westminster, and for Dr M'Hale to call himself Archbishop of Tuam, and the Government may, if it pleases – that is, if it is disposed to create a violent disturbance among the Irish Roman Catholics – prosecute the only party who systematically so offends. But it is quite legal for the parties to convey or receive property under these illegal titles, and all donations or bequests for supporting or endowing these dignities which Parliament declares illegal will be perfectly valid.' Sir John's answer to the enthusiasm he had blown up himself by an inadequate measure which was now so emasculated till it became as little acceptable to Protestant as to Romanist was a policy 'that we do not pretend to understand', and which, by implication, nobody else would understand either.

Of course things might have been different if the Government had acted only against the assumption of the titles in England, where Catholics were a minority and there had been no Catholic bishops for three hundred years, while leaving the Irish bishops who had been recognised for far longer than that to officiate as before over the spiritual and even temporal needs of the Catholic majority of the population. Why was this not done – and why (Mr Delane wondered for a moment) had *The Times* not drawn attention to the folly of the thing? Well, it could claim that it had never seen, even if it had never leadered on, the justice of the thing. Because, of course, with all their knowledge of the law, ministers and above all the Solicitor-General, the law officers of the Crown and even the Lord Lieutenant, Lord Clarendon, had been grossly negligent; all of a piece, in fact, with the utter inefficiency and blundering of Lord John Russell's administration from the moment the Pope had put a long-meditated and carefully prepared invasion into action in September. And *The Times* gave him notice that such a betrayal of duty forfeited the support it had given him since he took office back in 1846. . . .

21

'Well, Searle, so what does it amount to, eh?' Cardinal Archbishop Wiseman took up *The Times* and read out: '"After the abandonment of the Durham letter by the bill, and of the bill by the amendment, we think the wisest step would be to send the amendment to join its discarded predecessors. We were prepared – and so, we believe, were the people of England – to have supported any measure calculated to assert the dignity of our Crown and the inviolability of our constitution; but the Ecclesisastical Titles Bill is not worth, now, a single day's delay or a single hour's debate." Ha! *The Times* has struck its ensign, eh, my dear Monsignor? Do I not see the white flag fluttering from the mainmast of England's flagship? Is there anything else they can do?'

'No, Eminence,' replied Monsignor Searle, the Cardinal's secretary. 'Nothing whatever. Everybody admits that the remaining clause in the bill, which in theory empowers them to fine you a hundred pounds every time you use your title *coram populo*, will be a dead letter. The papers are already omitting the quotes when they refer to you as Archbishop. It'll never be enforced. It's a fig leaf to cover their political nakedness. The Government will debate it for a few weeks in committee, as parliamentary procedure requires, and Russell will hate every minute of it, and is probably even now wishing he could take *The Times*'s advice. Parliament will pass it for the sake of consistency, and then it will be forgotten. Your Eminence has trampled your enemies into the dust, and you can now freely go ahead with the real campaign, under the papal flag, the conversion of England to the true Faith.'

The Cardinal put the tips of his fingers together.

'Yes, Father Ignotius said this was the third invasion and conquest of England. The first was by Julius Caesar, the second by St Augustine, and now by me. His Holiness had publicly prayed for me to lead three million of our separated brethren back to Holy Church to begin with. To that end, I must take care to remind priests to emphasise to our new converts that it is a grave sin for any Catholic not to work tirelessly to convert his neighbours and his associates in business, politics or the professions. The same applies to their families. A good Catholic woman can make many converts. The rules on bringing up the children of mixed marriages as Catholics must be enforced by all priests. Then on to the total extinction of heresy in England. The final solution I may not live to see, but that which Monsignor Talbot and I began to plan five – six – years ago, has now been rewarded with its first success. By the grace of God.'

'By the grace of God.'

Both prelates crossed themselves. And then exchanged broad grins.

'Minto!'said Searle. 'Lord Minto! The great diplomat, who read nothing and signed everything, almost, you put before him. And he signed the deed that gives us the right to organise this mighty work. Oh, we remember Minto!'

'Oh yes, Minto! And it was Russell who sent him to us and who in effect countersigned that deed. And he reneged on it. But we have made him pay up like a cheating tradesman whose false weights have been exposed!' His Eminence's grin turned into a roar of laughter in which his private secretary dutifully joined.

'And there are first fruits already,' said the Cardinal. 'I have just been informed: Manning has submitted at last. And his friend, James Hope. Manning will gain us converts by the score. But our greatest prize has to be Gladstone. Greater even than Manning, in my view.'

'Greater than Manning? Why do you say that, Eminence?'

'Because Gladstone is going to be prime minister. Everyone has known that for years. Oh, not immediately. This parliamentary imbroglio, though it has served us well, will take some time to sort out. But he is the only man the Liberals and Free Traders have. They talk of Palmerston, but the Queen will never have him, never. As for Graham, our greatest ally in this battle, he's forfeited his chance by his very action in our favour. They must have a scapegoat and he'll be it, not Russell, when the Liberals look for someone to blame for their humiliation. As for the Tories, they have no chance: Manchester is too strong for them and they know it. Look at the way Lord Stanley steered them clear of taking office! Downy old aristocrat, he is.'

'You seem to have a wonderful grasp of the English power structure, Eminence.'

'I get most of it from Farm Street. The Jesuits know everybody and tell me. Of course that means I have to play ball with *them*.'

'And the Jesuit Fathers say it will be Gladstone? How soon?'

'That is in God's hands – but God has His sights on England. He gives us time to work on Gladstone first. Just think of it! A dedicated Catholic as prime minister! He will disestablish the Church of England. Give us our cathedrals back – who knows? *Finis coronat opus!*'

There was a tap on the door and the butler put his head round it. 'Father Numen, Yer Iminence.'

'Yes, show him in, Paddy. So he got your message, Searle? Ah, Father Newman, God be with you. Great news, what? Read *The Times* this morning?'

'I have, Your Eminence.' Father Newman knelt and kissed the ring. 'Delane has turned on his hero. Viciously. As was to be expected of a newspaper man: no time for losers – must pretend to infallibility.'

His Eminence chuckled.

'Well, Father, how are the lectures going? First you make them laugh, then you make them feel ashamed of reading rubbish like *Maria Monk and the Red Barn*. Monsignor Searle and I were talking about Gladstone. How will he be feeling now that Manning and Hope have finally come over? Have you seen him?'

'No, Your Eminence. Our former links have been quite severed, I fear. Not easy to restore, either.'

'But now he's lost Manning and Hope! Almost the last friends of his youth in Oxford. Surely that will have shaken him? He was just as appalled by the scandal of the Gorham case as they were. Laymen deciding Church doctrines. Phew!'

'Certainly. He must be suffering spiritual agonies. I . . . I pray for him. But you know the last time he saw Manning they were in church together, and when the moment to take communion came . . .'

'Oh yes, I've been told. Manning said "Come" to Gladstone and walked out. Gladstone stayed, still clinging to Pusey. But things are different now. We are established, Rome and England are reunited, the legal presence of the hierarchy advertises our growing power and influence. Gladstone is shrewd and will lean to the winning side.'

'With respect I fear not, Eminence. The Devil spoke in his ear at that moment and said, "Go and become a parish priest. Stay and become prime minister of England." He stayed. The Devil has no such power over others. No such option can be offered to tempt them – many are noblemen and women, already rich and powerful. They have nothing to risk and salvation to gain by coming over to us. We'll get many of them, but not, I fear, Gladstone. I know him.'

The Cardinal Archbishop heaved himself out of his chair. 'But now – surely now there need be no contradiction? We have won. We shall win, as you say, converts from the highest levels of society. Like Lord Feilding. It's going to be *fashionable* to convert to Rome. In a few years we shall be able to deliver a big Catholic vote to Catholic MPs. Gladstone has seen what we have done with the Irish MPs in the debate. They are now welded into an anti-English party. He'll appreciate that point.'

Father Newman stayed silent.

Searle said, 'We've won, but Gladstone may be influenced

LITTLE RED RIDING HOOD.

Having lost against Wiseman, *Punch* (unusually)
repeats the attack with the Roman Church as the big
bad wolf waylaying Little Red Riding Hood.

by the sheer size of the Protestant protest in terms of votes – mainly middle class and Liberal. Perhaps the Devil told him those votes were his if he acted the moral man of principle – and stayed in their Church, as spiky as he likes, so long as it isn't Roman. Your Eminence will appreciate that I'm only developing Father Newman's line of thought...'

'We take your point. But the tide has turned in England. I have met Gladstone and I mean to develop the acquaintance. Soon I shall be seen everywhere, people will defer to a prince of the church. Look how well they responded to my appeal for fair play and a fair hearing in November after the Guy Fawkes No Popery riots. I shall lecture, I shall blow away their prejudices against us – with Father Newman's invaluable help. I shall be very, very, *very* English even in my episcopal red. I shall be a veritable Mr Pickwick, all Dickensian geniality and fun. I shall explain that Rome's yoke is easy and her burden is light. And when I am received by the Queen, as I am by the other crowned heads of Europe, it will seem natural for a Catholic bishop to take his place in the House of Lords. Won't that impress a Catholic prime minister? Surely Gladstone will pass a law to seat me on the bench of bishops sooner or later? What do you think?'

*   *   *

'Here the conquering hero comes!
Blow, blow the trumpets! Beat, beat the drums...'

shouted the gathered funny men, so-called, of *Punch*, as John Leech entered the upper room of the Edinburgh Castle, to a great banging of spoons on the table and hooting through funnelled newspapers.

'Congratulations, congratulations,' shouted Lemon. 'Circulation figures show that your cut of Russell chalking up "No Popery" on Wiseman's door has put us up to over forty thousand. It has the whole town laughing, you must know it! Don't look so modest! The proprietors are delirious. *Punch*

130

has hit the bull's-eye. The Government might as well resign again. Champagne for John Leech!'

'All the same,' said Douglas Jerrold, 'the longest-running joke in our history is running out of steam. What do we do next? You're going to be hard to follow up, John.'

'I've got a tail-twister,' said Phiz. 'Remember that argument between Wiseman and Lady Morgan, how when the French took over Rome they found that St Peter's chair was not Roman at all, but a bit of booty from the Crusades as proved by the fact that it had the words "There is one God and Mahomet is His prophet" carved on it in Arabic. All those years the cardinals didn't know, they'd been too lazy to clean the chair and find it there. In the Middle Ages they never cleaned anything. I've done a sketch with Wiseman as Pope sitting on an Islamic throne. Look. Funny?'

'It'll pass,' said Thackeray. 'But don't forget Victoria sits on the Stone of Scone, which is Scottish. It makes her Scottish, of course, but perhaps St Peter's bogus chair gives the Pope the right to rule over Turkey. Jokes like that are not so funny any more. Hadn't we better come clean? We're beat, as Douglas said. Especially *Punch* and *The Times*. I've written Mr Punch a letter, as from a correspondent, so he don't confess his defeat openly, called "John Bull beaten". What it says is that if a lady smacks your face, you've an absolute right to reply, "Madam, I protest your behaviour is monstrous." It reserves our right to laugh at pretensions as antiquated as the priests of Jupiter, and invite Wiseman to set up a winking statue of the Virgin in the Strand to be winked back at by all, um, ladykillers who pass it.'

'Not that joke again, Thack, we've had it twice! It's what set Wiseman protesting at our ribald comments in the *Dublin Review* at Christmas. But now he's got the last laugh, let's face it.'

'Why not drop the whole thing? Wiseman made the point that we were jesting at religion itself, which is against *Punch*'s rules,' said Dicky Doyle. 'I'm a papist, as you know, and I've really had enough of this Pope-bashing. I'll damned well resign if you don't call it a day and take a defeat like a good sportsman. I'll have another pint of Meux.'

'Well, if we've lost,' said Jerrold, 'let's propose we have a medal struck, as the Pope did when the Huguenots were massacred.'

'The past is past,' said Doyle. 'For God's sake drop it.'

'I think it's John Russell we should tilt at,' said Thackeray. 'Look at him! The man's a standing joke, he and his whole incompetent family that runs this country! God help us if the Whigs are running it if a really big war ever breaks out. We'd be beaten all over again. Kaffirs they can just about manage, I suppose, but the French – Napoleon and Co. – my hat! They'd eat us. I'd like to write a dirge for him. Let's see now. Er, yes, I've got it, first verse, something like this.' He winked at them and intoned:

> 'Little Johnnie Russell
> Hid under a bustle,
> What could he do there,
> But look up and stare?'

The whole table burst into roars of ribald laughter, Doyle the papist loudest of all. 'Thack, oh, Thack, what should we do without you? said Lemon. 'It's good enough for *Punch*. If only we could print it. Ha, ha, ha!'

The editorial conference had got off to a mellow start.

22

Mr Delane looked unsmilingly at the *Punch* cartoon of Lord John as a street arab running away from Wiseman's episcopal palace in Soho after chalking 'No Popery' on the door. Lemon had hit the nail on the head again. Was the chapter now closed? Did *The Times* have to drop the story finally? Accept defeat? Grumble maybe, warn of the further aggression to come from Rome, but give up? It seemed so.

And what was the next crusade to be about? He could pour more scorn on the Whig clique who ran the country, and had failed it; but he must be careful not to encourage the Protectionists to try again. At the next ministerial crisis Dizzy might inveigle them into forming a ministry and seek to subvert Free Trade. *The Times* would not, could not, stand for that! The public wouldn't stand for it either. But that might never be in question. What, here and now, was *The Times* to lead the country on? The budget? The costly Kaffir War? Journalistically speaking, the outlook appeared bleak.

But wait. In his correspondence there had arrived a letter from a certain Mr Craven Fitzhardinge Berkeley to make public the fact that he was sending a petition to the House of Commons to release his stepdaughter, a Miss Augusta Talbot, a ward of court in Chancery, from a nunnery in which she was incarcerated and being pressured to become a nun. As Mr Delane read, his spirits rose. Mr Berkeley had broken a very interesting story of popish wickedness, intrigue and greed, the first-fruits of the new Vatican bishoprics and one which the cravenly abandoned clauses of the Ecclesiastical Titles Assumption Bill seemed uniquely designed to frustrate.

The poor girl, it seemed, had had a complicated and tragic life. Orphaned and an heiress, under the control not only of heartless relatives, the Earl and Countess of Shrewsbury, now England's senior Catholic nobles, but of her legal guardian, the callous and Jesuitical Dr Doyle, now the papist Bishop of Southwark, she had been brought up in the nunnery from infancy and now at eighteen was being duped by the ruthless abbess to become a postulant. Which meant that when, next year or soon afterwards, she dutifully took the black veil and renounced the world for ever, every penny of her property passed, under canon law, to the Church. To Dr Doyle and Nicholas Wiseman – £80,000! Oho!

The Cardinal had not finished with *The Times* yet! Not quite. Mr Delane sent for his legal expert, had the Shrewsbury record investigated and himself made enquiries in society drawing-rooms about the affair. Clearly a plot was afoot to rob and silence for ever an ignorant and inexperienced girl, unprotected save for the last-minute intervention of a step-father. She had been thoroughly indoctrinated by the abbess, Miss Jerningham, and allowed last year only briefly to visit London to be presented at court by the Shrewsburys, as befitted her rank, and also to be presented with a choice between marrying at once an oldish and (it was said) repulsive relative of the Salisbury family or being returned to the convent to be trained to renounce the world. The convent had seemed to Miss Talbot the less loathsome alternative.

And the one doubtless planned by Dr Doyle from the beginning, Mr Delane opined. 'A bold venture, but the prize was worth it,' commented *The Times*. 'A sum of eighty thousand pounds at one sweep and won with no greater labour than is involved in playing on the religious feelings of a young credulous girl who stood alone in the world without council, without defence and without protection. The persons who should have interposed have assisted in the practices of which she is now the victim.' By this *The Times* clearly pointed to the Shrewsburys, but not to them alone. What, it asked, is going on in respect of this ward – a sacred trust – in Chancery? For it now emerged that Mr Berkeley, after being refused a private talk with his stepdaughter by the abbess of the convent and having observed with his own eyes that Augusta was completely under that lady's thumb, had visited Lord Truro in person to demand a writ of habeas corpus – which the Lord Chancellor had refused. Hence his petition to Parliament.

Public interest was now satisfactorily aroused. Was the medieval monastic system to be reinstated in this country, just when even in Italy and Spain convents were being put under legal constraints?

This caused the 'pseudo Bishop of Clifton', one Mr Hendren, who controlled, under Dr Doyle's supervision, the nunnery and its abbess, to write to *The Times* denying that Augusta was not free to choose, so the Church could not be accused by the likes of Mr Delane of ulterior motives: Augusta had returned to the convent as a refugee from the worldliness which had disgusted her in London, and only if this caused her to choose the veil would her money go to the Church charities – which, unlike those of the wealthy state Church, were much underfunded. She was not a postulant at all. Enquiries from Dr Doyle admitted that she could not under Church rules be a boarder either, wearing lay attire and free to come and go as she chose. He, it appeared, was designing a special status to meet her case. But Lord Shrewsbury intimated that he had told Lord Truro during a visit to his mansion, Alton Towers, that Augusta was in the convent as a postulant, to which Lord Truro had nodded agreement; but Lord Truro denied this, because the court of Chancery could never allow its ward to have her entire future so tied up, let alone her money. Dr Hendren of Clifton further confused the issue by favouring *The Times* with the Church's rules for safeguarding postulants' freedom to withdraw, but warned (in Latin) that once they had agreed they were bound before God, and any further attempts to back out led to excommunication.

In a leader *The Times* presented the public with the story so far, and by printing side by side what Dr Doyle and Dr Hendren said, and what Miss Jerningham had said, demonstrated that the two bishops were contradicting each other and were proven liars out of their own mouths, while the abbess was an adept at moulding the minds of immature young girls. It went on to indict the Lord Chancellor himself for forgetting what he had said on the nod to Lord Shrewsbury and for failing to realise, when at last he *did* remember, that he had failed in his legal duty to protect vulnerable little girls like Augusta. The leading article implied that any of these great people could sue *The Times* for slander if they liked – which none of them did. Finally the court brought in a judgement that everybody except Lord Truro was to blame for letting down poor Augusta.

At which point Augusta herself intervened with a long and confused letter to Lord Truro, saying that she was not a postulant but everyone was ever so kind to her in the convent;

however, she felt that she should now leave it and place herself under the protection in London of someone whom Lord Truro could certify as respectable, but evidently not Dr Doyle, the Shrewsburys, Mr Berkeley or anybody else hitherto involved with her fate. It was at least clear that she was perfectly ready to go back to Vanity Fair, preferring (as *The Times* put it) to dance polkas until three in the morning – even at the risk of being asked for her hand in marriage by eligible gentlemen – to prayer and meditation on a low diet in those matutinal hours. . . .

Thus everybody involved (except Augusta) had his or her wrist smartly slapped by *The Times*, while the learned lawyers who had represented all the parties concerned had their fees paid out of the heiress's fortune. Lord Truro tried to make amends by acceding to Augusta's wishes and put her under the protection of a Catholic noblewoman of impregnable respectability, who turned out to be Lady Newburgh, an intimate of such Catholic personages as the Duke of Norfolk, the former premier Catholic nobleman.

And behold, in a matter of weeks a Catholic gentleman of the highest integrity who happened to be in need of £80,000 (less legal fees), had offered Miss Talbot his hand and she had accepted him – though probably without taking counsel of the Hon. Mrs Norton, who had just had another novel published about what happened to innocent girls with money (or to beautiful girls without) at the hands of suitors with engaging manners and conversational charm: s story that unquestionably had an autobiographical basis. So, as *The Times* discreetly reported the outcome, Augusta and her wealth duly disappeared behind the impenetrable veil of connubial bliss, after a relatively modest wedding at the Bavarian Embassy, into the possession of the Duke of Norfolk's younger son.

Nor did *The Times* leave matters there: it averred that this kind of spiritual blackmail was going on (though for smaller sums than £80,000) all over the country, where the victims were not protected by Chancery involvement, and that none of it could happen if the anti-papal bill had been allowed by the warring factions in Parliament to go through unaltered, as the people of England had wished, for then no money could get into the pockets of the new hierarchy at all.

Other newspapers were more cynical, saying that an orphan heiress was bound to be robbed and ruined by some plausible rogue, whether he wore clerical or lay trousers. This was unfortunate but inevitable, as it was of course unthinkable that a married woman should have control of her own money. The accepted legal authority on the laws of England, Sir William Blackstone, had made that abundantly clear.

Nevertheless *The Times* had given the case of Miss Talbot enough space and publicity to prompt Mr Lacy, MP for Bodmin, to attempt to bring in a bill to authorise magistrates to enter and inspect any closed religious house (they were now springing up all over England) and ask its inmates, especially young ladies, if they felt free to leave it, or did they need any help to do so? This produced an uproar in the House of Commons from the Irish benches, and the Earl of Arundel easily persuaded the House (and the Government, which depended on the Irish vote) to avoid another embarrassing passage of arms over religious and feminine freedoms, and reject the bill. Even *The Times* decided, in this matter, that discretion would be the better part of valour. Still, Mr Delane felt that *The Times* had adroitly jabbed the hierarchy in a tender spot.

The Cardinal, indeed, turned to another publicity-engendering subject to divert attention from the trials of Miss Talbot. In the role of a new Savonarola he attacked the Great Exhibition in a well-attended address, saying (*inter alia*), 'This year our metropolis will become the scene of such a display of magnificence and the gathering place of such multitudes as the world has perhaps never before witnessed. Its pilgrims will be the curious, the idle, the rich and the gay as much as the observant. Whatever is fair to the eye or alluring to the appetite will temptingly hang on every bough of this newly created paradise – who does not fear the increase of sin and vice? – all our usual temptations to folly, dissipation and worldliness will be increased, every snare that awaits youth will be multiplied. . . ?' And so on, fully worthy of an Exeter Hall killjoy, indeed of Colonel Sibthorpe himself.

(The worst was, however, averted: the Sabbatarian League insisted that the Exhibition should be closed on Sunday.)

Noticeable at the front of the audience were Lady Newburgh and her charge, Miss Talbot, who was heard to remark: 'But everybody is going, and so shall I.'

'So you shall, dear,' said Lady Newburgh. 'With your fiancé – why not? Lord Edward doesn't take sermons all that seriously.'

23

The Pre-Raphaelite Brotherhood formed a small disconsolate group hovering about the Royal Academy show in Trafalgar Square. Sometimes they broke up into ones or twos, and then coalesced again before one of their own paintings, or somebody else's. Sometimes a wan but exceedingly beautiful girl with masses of coppery-gold hair drifted with them. She was never heard to say anything. The others murmured to each other mournfully or sought to overhear the comments of the other visitors looking at their pictures.

They were considerably irked by the much greater attention being given to a nearby life-sized portrait in oils of His Eminence Cardinal Archbishop of Westminster, Nicholas Wiseman DD.

'Beautiful! Lifelike! Such a compassionate expression! Yet so determined, so – so virile!' said not a few of the ladies. 'So that's him, is it?' snorted some of the men. 'Proper medieval ruffian, ain't he? Flauntin' his gewgaw cross and his robes and red hat. And no expense spared in the painting, either! Frame alone cost a fortune. Grrrr!'

'And the hat wouldn't fit his head. And the robes are made of thick cardboard,' murmured Holman Hunt.

'And the red would come out black in that light,' growled

Rossetti. 'Who's this Brigstocke feller? He can't paint for toffee.'

Two young men stationed themselves before *Ophelia*, quizzed it with mock artists' expressions, turned to face John Millais and sniggered.

Millais glowered. 'You laughed, sir. If you were to live to the age of Methuselah, and you were to improve every day of your life more than you will in the entire course of it, you would never achieve anything fit to compare to this picture.'

They laughed and strolled on. 'Touchy feller, ain't he?'

'I didn't mean to explode,' Millais said to Hunt. 'Just couldn't help it! Have you noticed? Half of them are merely mouthing what *The Times* said about us.' He drew the creased cutting from his pocket. He read it in a low voice to Hunt, who had read it already but listened just the same as though to his own death sentence from a judge under the black cap:

'"We cannot censure as strongly as we desire to do that strange disorder of the mind or the eyes which continues to rage with unabated absurdity among a class of juvenile artists who style themselves the Pre-Raphaelite brethren. Their faith seems to consist of an absolute contempt for perspective and the known laws of light and shade, an aversion to beauty in every shape, and a singular devotion to the minute accidents of their subject including every degree of deformity. The public may fairly require that such offensive jests should not continue to be exposed as specimens the waywardness of these artists who have lapsed into the infancy of their profession." – Ugh!'

'The trouble is that people believe that *The Times knows*,' said Millais, 'and is always right. Why should *The Times* know anything about art? But this penny-a-liner does say it in language that ordinary people can understand. They say, "Ah yes, how true" and then *see* it as true. "This morbid infatuation which sacrifices truth, beauty, and genuine feeling to mere eccentricity deserves no quarter." '*The Times* is determined to smash us.'

'Yes, but students at the Academy had a row with their professor for talking like *The Times* about us,' said Rossetti.

'Talking! Why, my father in the City is being laughed at for his son's public howlers,' said Holman Hunt.

At that moment Coventry Patmore burst into the room, causing visitors to turn their heads and look affronted. 'He's done it, you fellows – you haven't seen today's *Times*? Thought they'd done with you? No, they have not, or rather you've not done with *them*. Just read this – Ruskin's letter, last page. He's praised you to the skies and smashed the critics. Here. . . .'

They crowded round him and nearly tore the paper as they drank it in like thirsting men finding an oasis in the desert.

'"There is not a single study of drapery, be it in large works or small" – that's the RAs – "which for perfect truth, power and finish can be compared for an instant with the black sleeve of the Julia, or with the the chain mail of the Valentine of Mr Hunt's picture, or with the white draperies on the table of Mr Millais's *Mariana* . . ."'

'Listen to that! So much for cardboard canonical robes,' laughed Hunt.

'And this: ". . . the water plant *Alisma Plantago* as I have never seen it so well drawn: for a mere botanical study of the water-lily and several other garden flowers the picture would be invaluable to me and I wish it were mine . . ."'

'Golly, he'll buy our pictures, he, the mighty Ruskin! Perhaps he'll buy the whole *Ophelia*,' crooned Millais.

'And listen to this, O Brothers,' said Patmore: '"If they do not suffer themselves to be driven by harsh or careless criticism into rejection of the ordinary means of obtaining influence over the minds of others, they may, as they gain experience, lay in our England the foundations of a school of art nobler than the world has seen for three hundred years."'

'And so much for *The Times*,' said Hunt, spreading his hands.

They read and read and turned to each other, awed.

'You have won,' said Patmore. 'You'll see. You've put something up here in Trafalgar Square the equal of anything they've got to exhibit over at the Crystal Palace. It will be so recognised, too, I swear it.'

'Let's get out of here and start drinking.' Rossetti was saying

THE SHIPWRECKED MINISTERS SAVED BY THE GREAT EXHIBITION STEAMER.

The Whig government's prestige totally shipwrecked, Lord John Russell sends an SOS for rescue to the big steamer, *Great Exhibition 1851*.

it, as solemnly as though he meant to lead them in prayers in St Martin-in-the-Field.

Mr Delane was writing a letter: 'I am afraid I must disagree with you on the validity of your column of last week after the reproofs levelled at your criticisms by the eminent author of *Modern Painters*. This I find is the universal view. He has discovered greatness and you have lost *The Times* the privilege of first announcing its emergence to the public. You have disappointed the public's feelings of reliance on *The Times* art critic, and it is now impossible for us to hail this event in a leading article, which you would normally have the privilege of writing for us. In such circumstances I feel sure you will agree that that the only honourable course is for you to provide me with your written resignation from that office.'

24

For months everything had pointed to the success of the Great Exhibition. Londoners had watched the colossal glass case grow upwards amazingly, enclosing whole trees and infuriating property owners on the verges of Hyde Park. It was a free show and nothing went in accordance with Colonel Sibthorpe's doom-laden predictions. All the components, wood, ironware, glass, arrived to schedule and were thrown upwards by an army of workmen. Rain had not got through the roof, hailstones had not smashed it, winds had not blown it down, the flooring had been stamped on by a platoon of guardsmen and had not given way. Uncountable tonnages of numbered crates, bales, packages and sacks had been swallowed up inside; there had been no thefts and nobody had been murdered outside by thugs, socialists and revolutionaries: Colonel Sibthorpe grew angrier daily. Even the suggestion that the Queen for safety's sake should not attend the opening had been quashed by a severe leading article in

The Times: trust the people! The suggestion that if she attended the opening the season ticket-holders should be kept out until she had left safely was shouted down.

The flags of all the nations had been broken out along the roofage; the royal standard was hoisted above the great transept; the bands played, the fountains played, the rain stopped; the sun shone, the machinery roared, the organs and orchestras boomed Mendelssohn alternately with the national anthem, the cannons fired, the traffic completely jammed, balloons were swept overhead by favourable breezes, the aeronauts in their baskets cheering and waving yet more flags. Joy was unconfined. Exhibitions there had been – yes; but never one like this, international and proclaiming Year One of an era of international peace and goodwill (catalogues had been printed in English, French and German). British exhibits took up two-thirds of the acreage, the rest one third. Incontestably, Britain was cock of the walk.

So the Prince (and Mr Paxton) had triumphed against the odds. With his adoring queen on his arm the Prince led the procession of everybody who was anybody in the entire perambulation past six thousand exhibits: the once and only king, to all intents and purposes.

An uninvited mandarin from a junk anchored somewhere off Wapping Old Stairs slipped past the functionaries marshalling the dignitaries for the address, and did the kotow before Her Majesty: a happy omen for burgeoning trade in tea, opium and missionary endeavour.

Mysterious Japan sent nobody and nothing.

*

'They'll never turn you out now after this triumph, even if it is Albert's,' said Lady Russell, fairly far forward in the precedence which governed the procession. 'Everybody will be talking about it for weeks and it will tide you over to the recess.'

The Prime Minister nodded cheerfully. 'Quite right, Fanny. Mind you, after so many defeats in this rabble of a House and the loss of our best whip, I've had my doubts. But the nation's triumphs are always credited to the government of the day and not the Opposition. . . .' He managed in passing to smirk at his reflection in his new court dress in a boudoir-glass mounted in an elaborately embellished bronze frame supported by two naked nymphs and illuminated by baroque oil-lamps depending from chains hung from the beaks of two heraldic eagles: made in Birmingham.

*

Glancing at the Archimedeean Root Washer as the procession traipsed past it, Mr Disraeli said mournfully, 'The whole thing is an advertisement for Free Trade. Where is the toil and sweat of the noble land-owner, collecting his rents and improving his broad acres by hunting over them, given his due? Most of the exhibits are made in factories and towns. Exhibits from abroad advertise the markets still to be conquered by Manchester. How on earth am I to persuade my followers of this? Protection is dead. Dead *and* damned.'

'But the fountains are so pretty,' said Mrs Dizzy.

'Made in Birmingham,' said the Protectionist leader in the Commons.

*

'There it is, my great crucifix, dethroned in a corner,' snarled Mr Pugin, as they entered the dark Mediaeval Court. 'Damn them to hell!'

'Steady, steady on, Mr Pugin,' said his companion, a large clerical person, who was in disguise, his pectoral cross hidden. 'It is a most beautiful piece of work, we must have it to preside over the chancel of Westminster Cathedral, to the glory of God, and as your own memorial.'

'But I designed it to preside over the glasshouse for a season, up in the roof, to sanctify this unholy place, this sepulchre of good taste, and to claim it, in a sense for the Faith, Your Eminence, to symbolise your conquest of the Anglican heresy. But the dolts on the committee rejected it for that very reason. Said it might provoke a riot.'

'It is here, all the same,' said the big cleric. 'The hanging committee of the Academy tried to keep out Brigstocke's fine portrait of myself for fear of public ructions, too! But it's there, and very eye-catching it is! . . . Ah, my dear Lord. . . .'

A lady and a gentleman had entered the dim recess of the fourteenth century and, after a startled look, knelt to kiss the episcopal ring, murmured something and, their Catholic duty done, in evident embarrassment hurriedly withdrew, without asking any further blessing.

'Good gracious, Eminence, who were they?' said Mr Pugin, taken aback.

'Lord Edward Fitzalan-Howard,' growled the Cardinal, 'and his intended, Miss Augusta Talbot. Plus her eighty thousand pounds, by rights intended for the Church! What a family, the Norfolks! They snatched her from under our noses, that infernal Chancery court fixed it, much to his apostate father's amusement, no doubt. To provide for his impecunious youngest son, who has to live in a hole called Glossop! Glossop! Well, she can join him there! But if they want me to marry them, they'll have to give the Church a moiety of the dower. His brother, Henry – the Earl of Arundel, you know, when he succeeds his ghastly old father – will see us right. A true son of the Church!'

*

Miss Florence Nightingale was looking critically at the patent invalid bedstead, which at the touch of a lever lifted the body so that the bed could be made up under the patient, and the head or back raised so that the patient could recline in any position best suited to his injury, all by a single nurse.

'It looks practical, as an idea,' said Miss Nightingale, 'saving the nurse's time . . . but I wonder how well it would work in a hospital in actual practice?'

'Oh, Flo, do come on,' said Miss Parthenope Nightingale. 'Mother and I want to look at the koh-i-noor. . . .'

Mr and Mrs Coventry Patmore were gazing entranced at the statue, in Parian ware, of Una sitting side-saddle on her guardian lion which was impatiently pawing its plinth. The composition was given the title *Purity*: a wreath of white lilies and a white dove clung pillion behind Una to the draperies which Una was in the process of coquettishly letting slip off the lion's back.

'My own angel, it symbolises our perfect union,' said Mr Patmore. 'Only Una is not as beautiful as you are . . . when attired only in your maidenly beauty. . . . A highly poetical piece . . . as good as Woolmer's medallion of you, angel mine.'

'Yes, my dear lion,' said Mrs Patmore. 'Shall we go and look at the koh-i-noor now?'

*

The Revd and Mrs Charles Kingsley were looking at the American sculptor Hiram Power's statue of a Greek slave-girl, deprived of her clothing (Mr Power explained in a label) and exposed for sale by some wealthy Eastern barbarian, her face a study of scornful rejection, shame and disgust. As 'necessary accessories, though not historically correct,' Mr Power added, her wrists were constrained by pendant chains.

'If he'd carved it in ebony instead of marble,' said Mrs Kingsley, 'it might have symbolised the slavery in the South.'

'Yes,' said the Revd Kingsley. 'You are always right. But I confess, my love, that the alabaster white in the representation of a woman is most evocative of the feelings of holy Christian love . . .'

'Yes,' said Mrs Kingsley, 'I do want to see this new gas cooking stove in the catalogue. I wonder if one could be fitted into the rectory kitchen?'

*

Mr Matthew Arnold, poet and HM Inspector of Schools, was standing with his arm round the waist of his fiancée, Miss Lucy Wightman, admiring a child's ornamental cot in cast brass, with the figure of an angel introduced at the head to support the drapery (and bless the occupant, presumably). She squeezed his hand and they moved on to the four-poster brass bedstead in the Elizabethan style by Winfield of Birmingham, at which she squeezed his hand again.

'Only three weeks and we are married, Flu – can you imagine it?' said the poet. His fiancée squeezed his hand yet again.

*

Mr George Henry Lewes and Miss Mary Ann Evans, standing side by side, were examining specimens of bookbinding with massive emblematic toolings and discussing the novels she hoped to write.

'I shall have to adopt a masculine *nom de guerre*,' she said, 'like Miss Brontë. What do you think of "George Eliot", George?'

'I love it,' said Mr Lewes.

*

Dr Ashburner had found himself in the German section, where he had become excited by the possibilities of the Morse code in telegraphy.

'You admit that mesmerism is a genuine phenomenon which is of utility in medicine,' he was arguing with Mr Herbert Spencer. 'As you saw yourself when my passes, a magnetic phenomenon, over Mr Carlyle's constipated bowel gave him prompt relief. Yet you reject the operation of spirit activity as demonstrated in table-tapping, what we call the higher phenomena of electro-biology. Spirit messages are invisible like electric messages along the railway telegraph wires. But a few years ago you would have deemed them impossible, yet they spanned the Channel until the wires unfortunately broke. Well, spirit messages are weak just because we too are taking time to evolve mechanisms to pick them up. So far we can only converse by asking them to respond with one tap for "yes" and two for "no" as we read out the alphabet from A to Z. Imagine how slow that is: when asking a spirit "Who are you?" just to get its response to the first

147

letter, W, we have to work through almost the entire alphabet, and so to H and then to O, a tap for "no", two for "yes". Now all we have to do is teach the spirits the code. Light tap, loud tap for A, loud tap, three light taps for B and so on. The message comes through like a telegraphic signal. Deny that's scientific proof, if you can?'

'I won't deny it if I hear it,' said Mr Spencer. 'Let me know when you've trained a spirit to talk to me in Morse code.'

*

Earlier in the German section the Prince and the Duke lingered over the exhibit of a firm in Essen called Krupp.

'The committee asked exhibitors to confine their exhibits to objects illustrative of the arts of peace, not war,' said the Prince. 'But Prussia has done the exact opposite, Duke. It's nothing but military and naval hardware. The steel barrel of this six-pounder gun, I am told, is tougher than anything we can make. Compared with our six-pounder, that should mean it takes a heavier charge, has a greater muzzle velocity and a longer range. What do you think?'

'Balls,' said the British Commander-in-Chief.

*

Mrs Monckton Milnes had seen nothing much. Mr Milnes had spent the entire tour of the exhibits meeting people.

'My dear Earl, my dear Viscount, my dear Lady Palmerston, my dear Chancellor, my dear Mrs Carlyle, my dear Bulwer Lytton, my dear Dickens, my dear Lord Shaftesbury, my dear Mr Disraeli, my dear Greville'. It went on and on. 'Allow me to introduce my wife, yes, thank you, we have only just got married. . . .' It went on and on and *on.*

'How do you do, how do you do, how do you do. . . .' Curtsy, curtsy, curtsy. . . . 'Yes, isn't it perfectly astounding, marvellous, wonderful . . .' reiterated the new mistress of Fryston Hall, as, her headache getting steadily worse, she squared her shoulders to meet the enemy's assaults.

By accident they met at the Fountain.

'Ah, Thackeray. I don't think you've met my wife yet? Fanny, this is Mr Thackeray of *Punch*, who thinks he's the Poet Laureate.'

'How do you do, Mrs Tennyson. Allow me to introduce my daughters, Anny and Minny. It was, I assure you, ma'am, *The Times* that mistook me for your illustrious husband. When I pointed out their error they merely said they could not keep the column waiting for the Exhibition ode and I had twenty minutes to fill it. Deadlines are deadlines for us poor slaves of the press.'

'It was a damn bad poem, Thackeray.'

'It was your official duty to write it, Tennyson. That's what laureates are for.'

'I had more important business on hand. Good-day, Thackeray. Come along, my dear.'

'Good-day, Tennyson. Your servant, ma'am.'

'Why was it a damn bad poem, Father? I liked it.'

'You must never say "damn", Minny. Promise me. Unless you want me to have you whipped, which I would hate to have to do. I think it was a good poem, even if it was official issue. . . . Now, then:

"But yesterday a naked sod,
The dandies sneered from Rotten Row,
And cantered o'er it to and fro,
And see! 'tis done! As though 'twere by a wizard's rod,
A blazing arch of lucid glass
Leaps like a fountain from the grass,
To meet the sun!"

'And eighteen more stanzas of the same standard quality. Ten pounds. A column and a half. So put that in your pipe and smoke it, Mr Laureate.'

'I like it, Father, too,' said Anny. 'I shall learn it by heart.'

'Tell you what, my dear little women, I bet you each a

sixpence that the first person we meet who knows us and speaks to us, will congratulate me on it.'

A minute later Mr Monckton Milnes congratulated him on it.

*

Colonel Sibthorpe was itching to make as much hay inside the palace as he had made outside it, but he had sworn never to enter it. The only thing to do was to return in dudgeon to Lincoln. On his arrival five and a half hours later he gave the engine-driver a severe reprimand for being eight minutes late. Colonel Sibthorpe prided himself on having opposed in the House every railway bill since the Liverpool & Manchester; but as they had all got through he felt he had a right at least to insist on their keeping proper time, as the mail coaches had done when the journey took two and a half days.

*

Mr Delane found himself looking at the Italian exhibits. He was examining the mosaics sent from Rome, when an expostulatory cry rang out behind him.

'Look at it! It's a scandal! It's not Italian! It's three separate states that ought to be Italy – Tuscany, Sardinia and Rome. And can Sicily offer nothing? Our noble country can only rake up this mishmash for the Exhibition. And where is the glass of Venice and the silk of Milan? Oh, they're here, but not in Italy – they're in Austria! The greatest exhibit in the Exhibition is the wounds of Italy, the cry of Italy for Risorgimento echoes through this wonderful building and the five flags which masquerade as representative of Italy shrink in shame amidst the mass of honourable bunting that adorns the roof!'

Mr Delane turned to find the owner of this rhetoric haranguing several English ladies and immediately was drawn in as a witness.

'Is it not so, sir, if I may address you with so little ceremony?

150

I am Giuseppe Mazzini. You may have heard of me? May I be privileged to know your name, sir?'

Mr Delane acknowledged the other's bow. Disengaging himself from the encounter he said, 'Sir, you are speaking to *The Times.*'

SOME YEARS LATER

Cardinal Archbishop Wiseman was resting in his morning-room in his private residence in York Place. He never felt well nowadays and a heart attack could carry him off at any time. He knew that delicately phased, high-level ecclesiastical negotiations were afoot as to who was to be his successor. But he didn't care much. The obvious candidate was Manning, who had long been his aide, and who laboured under the illusion that he controlled the diocese. There he was wrong. The Cardinal was and would be till he drew his last breath. Whoever then got the mitre would have to cope with the endless quarrels of his bishops, so heavily imbued with the ingrained Anglo-Saxon, one could almost say Anglican, contentiousness that Rome had found so unexpectedly trying. The only way to cope with it was to retain absolute power – to have the last word. Like the Pope.

He rang his handbell. Monsignor Searle and Canon Morris appeared. He greeted them. How could they serve His Eminence? 'Get me someone to take dictation will you, my friends? I want to write a letter to the Holy Father.' They demurred politely. Was such a step wise? Would it not overtax his strength? What was there to be said just at this moment? Could he tell them the outline and let them make a draft? 'Just send me a stenographer,' he replied, with slight emphasis on the word 'send'.

'Most Holy Father,' he dictated. 'My time is near, as your most kind and gracious enquiries about my health show that you know and sympathise. I am quite ready, my mind is clear and at peace. I find myself reviewing my work here

152

since you laid your charge upon me, nearly fourteen years ago. One remaining point troubles me somewhat. I expected to fulfil your hopes expressed to a deputation of English converts in Rome that once the Lord had brought to nothing but humiliation the English Government's effort to strangle the hierarchy I would lead into the Church three millions of my fellow-countrymen still separated from the Holy See to the end that I might cause them all to enter, even to the last man.

'I have never forgotten those words, and it is right that I should express to you at last my remorse at my failure to fulfil them. In those fourteen years we have not yet reached one million. Conversions have risen from about twenty a year to over two hundred a year, but even with twelve hundred priests at work instead of the fifty we started with, we are still far behind schedule. On current projections we shall hardly reach it until the next century. Though the converts have brought with them a rich harvest of charitable contributions to the Holy See, Your Holiness was entitled to count on far more in view of England's ever-growing (if undeserved) wealth, luxury and power to tax the labouring millions of her increasing empire as the workshop of the whole world.

'Our opponents, the Anglican Church and the sects that have broken off from it, take their cut out of this yearly harvest of English skill, invention and scientific discovery. But it is a field sown with tares as well as corn. We (and they) have a new opponent. Science itself is spreading infidelity and doubt, beginning to be worshipped even, as a new religion of reason and revelation. The need to keep our flock uncontaminated by this new paganism is as urgent as it may prove difficult. Your Syllabus of Modern Errors will reinforce the Church's traditional teaching, but the impact of those errors, especially science, on the reservoir of converts to be harvested, troubles me. At the head of this new doctrine stands a man called Darwin who, with his own adherents, is explaining the creation of the world, and even of man – of Adam and Eve – as a purely natural evolutionary process. Such teaching has the effect of releasing men from the fetters of original sin, and I need not expatiate, Most Holy Father, on how such ideas, if they spread beyond the present small class of *cognoscenti*, would damage the discipline of our congregation.

'So far it is but a cloud the size of a man's hand, but I wish to add my concern in case it can lend urgency to the defences being prepared by the Propaganda and the Holy Inquisition. . . .'

He rang his bell and Searle was at his side in a moment.

'Have this letter engrossed, please, and add any of, the, er, proper compliments to the Holy Father I may have left out.'

He leaned back in his chair as the stenographer bowed and withdrew.

'You know, Monsignor, I had the most extraordinary dream last night. It just does not leave me, it was so vivid. You remember I visited Canterbury Cathedral a few months ago. I think that may have suggested it. I dreamed I was back there, as before, in mufti. And there by the desecrated tomb of the blessed St Thomas I saw the Pope kneeling in prayer side by side with the Archbishop of Canterbury! As I gazed at them, a terrible commotion broke out at the cathedral doors, which were locked. A great horde of women outside were hammering on it, screaming and yelling, in unearthly tones, to be let in. I gathered, in the way one does in dreams, that what the Pope and the Archbishop were praying for was that God would keep them out!

'A nightmare, Searle: I woke up in terror, sweating. Has it a meaning? I ask myself. Perhaps it warns how inadvisable it is for a Catholic to enter Anglican precincts . . . what do you think?'